I0843326

Voices of the Civil War

Barry Robbins

Talk+Tell

Dedication

To Pam, my caregiver extraordinaire, without whom this work would not have been possible. Words cannot express my gratitude.

Contents

Prelude

Dear Reader,

In your hands, you hold a unique chronicle of the American Civil War. "Voices of the Civil War" is not a traditional history book, but rather a tapestry of experiences woven from the threads of countless lives touched by this pivotal conflict.

The pages that follow contain letters, speeches, journal entries, newspaper articles, and personal reflections that bring to life the tumultuous years of 1861-1865. While these documents capture the essence of real historical events and figures, it is important to note that they are not verbatim transcriptions of primary sources. Instead, they are carefully crafted representations, designed to convey the spirit, emotions, and perspectives of those who lived through these extraordinary times.

The voices you will encounter—from presidents and generals to common soldiers and civilians—speak with authenticity, even if the exact words are not those recorded in historical archives.

This approach allows us to explore the human side of history, to feel the hopes, fears, and convictions of those who shaped and were shaped by the Civil War. It offers a window into the hearts and minds of individuals caught in the maelstrom of a nation divided.

As you read, I invite you to immerse yourself in these voices from the past. Let them guide you through the complexities of a war that redefined a nation. Experience the conflict not just as a series of battles and political decisions, but as a profound human drama that continues to resonate with us today.

May these voices speak to you across the centuries, offering insights into our shared history and the enduring spirit of the American people.

Pre-War Years

Chapter 1

A Necessary Evil

A Georgia Planter Defends Slavery, 1819

The humid Georgia air clings to my skin as I stand on the veranda of Magnolia Grove, surveying the sea of cotton that stretches to the horizon. The rhythmic sound of hoes striking earth mingles with the distant singing of field hands, a melody both mournful and defiant. I, Jonathan Calhoun Whitaker, inhale deeply, the rich scent of soil and green cotton bolls filling my lungs.

"Mr. Whitaker," a voice interrupts my reverie. I turn to see Tom, my overseer, his face glistening with sweat. "The new shipment of slaves has arrived."

I nod, suppressing a sigh. "Very well, Tom. I'll be down shortly."

As I descend the steps, my wife Catherine calls from the doorway, "Jonathan, do be gentle with them. They must be frightened half to death."

I offer her a reassuring smile, but inwardly, I bristle. These abolitionists up North have even my wife questioning our way of life. They don't understand the burden we bear, the delicate balance we must maintain.

At the slave quarters, a group of dejected Africans huddles together, eyes downcast. A young woman clutches a baby to her chest, her body trembling.

"Welcome to Magnolia Grove," I announce, trying to infuse my voice with warmth. "You'll find that if you work hard and follow our rules, you'll be treated fairly here. We'll provide for your needs—food, shelter, purpose. Many of you may even find salvation through Christ under our guidance."

As I speak, I notice an older man among them, his eyes meeting mine with an unsettling defiance. I make a mental note to have Tom keep a close eye on that one.

Later, as I sip whiskey on the veranda, my brother-in-law James joins me. "Heard about the ruckus up in Missouri?" he asks, settling into a chair.

I nod grimly. "They want to enter the Union as a slave state. And they should. We must maintain the balance in Congress, lest those Northern agitators gain too much power."

James frowns. "But Jonathan, don't you ever wonder if they might be right? If slavery is truly as evil as they claim?"

I set down my glass, anger flaring in my chest. "Don't tell me you've been listening to those abolitionists, James. Our entire way of life depends on this institution. Without slavery, who would tend these fields? Who would harvest the cotton that clothes the nation and fills our coffers?"

"But at what cost?" James persists. "The human cost, I mean."

I stand, pacing the veranda. "The cost of progress is always high, James. Yes, slavery is a brutal system. I don't deny that. But it's a necessary evil. These Africans...they're not like us. They need our guidance, our civilization. And in return, they provide the labor that builds our nation's wealth."

I pause, gazing out at the fields where the last workers are finishing for the day. "The Bible itself speaks of slavery. Are we to argue with divine providence? No, this is the natural order of things."

James is quiet for a long moment. "I hope you're right, Jonathan. For all our sakes."

As the sun sets over Magnolia Grove, casting long shadows across the cotton fields, I can't shake a feeling of unease. Change is coming, that much is certain. The debate over Missouri's statehood is just the beginning.

I drain my glass, steeling my resolve. Our way of life is under threat, and I'll be damned if I'll let it be destroyed without a fight. The abolitionists don't see the bigger picture—in their pursuit of lofty ideals, they'd tear apart the very fabric of our society.

No, slavery must continue. It's the foundation upon which our world is built. Remove it, and everything we know comes tumbling down.

As darkness falls, the sound of singing drifts up from the slave quarters. A chill runs down my spine, and for a moment, I wonder if James might be right. But I push the thought away. We're too far along this path to turn back now. God help us all if we're wrong.

Chapter 2

The Stain on Our Republic

A Boston Abolitionist Speaks Out, 1819

The chill Boston air bites at my face as I hurry along the cobblestone streets, my breath forming small clouds in the fading twilight. Gas lamps flicker to life, casting long shadows across the redbrick buildings. My satchel, heavy with freshly printed pamphlets, thumps against my side with each step.

As I approach the meeting hall, a group of well-dressed gentlemen exits a nearby tavern. One sneers in my direction. "There goes Garrison, off to stir up trouble again!"

I straighten my back and walk on. My name is Elias Winthrop Garrison, and I've long since grown accustomed to such derision. The son of a wealthy merchant, I've sacrificed my inheritance and social standing for a greater cause: the immediate abolition of slavery.

Inside the hall, the air is thick with the scent of lamp oil and damp wool. My fellow abolitionists mill about, their faces etched with determination. I spot young William Lloyd Garrison (no relation) setting up a display of anti-slavery literature.

"Elias!" he calls out. "Have you heard the latest from Missouri?"

I shake my head, and William's face darkens. "They're pushing hard for admission as a slave state. If they succeed..."

"Then the balance tips further toward barbarism," I finish grimly.

As I prepare my notes for tonight's speech, my mind wanders to the plantation I visited in Virginia last summer. The image of a young slave girl, her back crisscrossed with whip scars, still haunts my dreams. It was that moment that transformed me from a gradualist to an immediatist.

The meeting begins, and I take my place at the podium. Faces both black and white look up at me expectantly.

"Friends, fellow seekers of justice," I begin, my voice ringing out in the packed hall. "We gather here tonight in the shadow of a great moral crisis. Even now, forces in Missouri seek to expand the poisonous reach of slavery into new territories."

A murmur of anger ripples through the crowd.

"The arguments of the slaveholders sicken me," I continue, my voice rising with passion. "They speak of economic necessity, of paternalistic care for their 'property.' But I have seen the reality with my own eyes—the whipping posts, the separation of families, the denial of basic human dignity. No amount of biblical misinterpretation or pseudo-scientific racism can justify such cruelty!"

"Here, here!" someone shouts, and a smattering of applause breaks out.

But not all are convinced. An older gentleman stands up. "Mr. Garrison, while I abhor slavery as much as you, isn't your approach too radical? Shouldn't we work within the system, advocate for gradual emancipation?"

I take a deep breath, tamping down my frustration. I've heard this argument too many times. "Sir, how many more must suffer while we wait for slavery to die a 'natural death'? Every day we delay, more families are torn apart, more souls are crushed under the weight of bondage. The time for half-measures has passed."

As I continue my speech, outlining our plans to flood Congress with petitions and to establish a network to help escaped slaves, I can see the fire of conviction growing in the eyes before me. Yes, they label us radicals, fanatics even. But I know in my heart that history will prove us right.

After the meeting, as we clear away the chairs, William approaches me. "Powerful words, Elias. But...do you ever worry that our actions might provoke a violent response from the South?"

I pause, the weight of his question settling on my shoulders. "I do, William. But what choice do we have? For as long as one person remains in chains, none of us is truly free. The stain of slavery darkens the soul of our nation, and only by washing it clean can we truly call ourselves the land of the free."

As I step out into the cold Boston night, my resolve is stronger than ever. The path ahead is long and fraught with danger, but we must persist. The very future of our republic hangs in the balance.

Chapter 3

The Missouri Compromise

Henry Clay: The Great Compromiser, 1820

On this warm evening in the summer of 1820, the weight of the nation rests heavy on my shoulders as I sit in my study, quill in hand. The Missouri question has been settled—for now. As I gaze out the window towards the Capitol, bathed in the fading light of this momentous year, I can't help but wonder if we've truly averted a crisis or merely postponed it. My heart is a maelstrom of relief, doubt, and a gnawing fear for our nation's future.

They're calling me "The Great Compromiser" in the halls of Congress. A flattering title, to be sure, but one that comes with a great burden. It fell to me, Henry Clay, a son of Kentucky straddling the divide between North and South, to forge a path through this impasse.

I recall the day, scarcely a year ago, when Missouri's petition for statehood landed on Congress's desk like a lit powder keg. The debates that followed were fierce, the stakes unimaginably high. One wrong move, one misplaced word, and our young nation might have torn itself apart. Many nights, I found myself pacing these very floors, the ghost of my father seeming to watch me. "A man must stand for something," he used to say. But what does one do when standing firm might break the very thing you're trying to protect?

The solution we crafted is far from perfect. Missouri will enter the Union as a slave state, balanced by Maine's admission as a free state. We've drawn a line across the 36°30' parallel, declaring that slavery shall not exist above it in the Louisiana Purchase territories. It's a precarious balance, but it's the best we could achieve. Even now, I feel the weight of the chains we've allowed to remain, the price of our fragile peace.

I hear the whispers already. Some say I've betrayed the cause of freedom, others claim I've undermined the rights of the South. Their words sting more than I care to admit. The truth, as always, lies somewhere in between. As Speaker of the House, I couldn't stand idly by and watch our Union crumble. We needed time—time for cooler heads to prevail, time for our nation to grow stronger.

Yet, even as the ink dries on this compromise, I fear we've merely bandaged a wound that will fester. Slavery, that great moral and political evil, as Jefferson calls it, remains a cancer at the heart of our republic. This compromise may buy us peace for now, but for how long? The faces of the enslaved I've seen in my travels haunt my dreams, their unspoken accusations echoing in my ears.

I've done what I believe is right for our nation, but the cost to my political aspirations may be dear. The presidency has long been my ambition, but in reaching across the aisle to secure this compromise, I may have alienated too many to ever reach that lofty goal. The bitter irony is not lost on me—that in trying to unite the nation, I may have divided my own path to its highest office.

Still, as I retire for the night, I take solace in knowing that our Union stands intact. We've weathered this storm, but I fear it's only the first of many to come. May God grant us the wisdom and courage to face the challenges ahead. And may He forgive us for the hard choices we've had to make in the name of preservation.

Chapter 4

The Little Giant's Gambit

Stephen Douglas and the Compromise of 1850

Washington City, September 1850

The Senate chamber, still thick with the acrid smell of tobacco smoke and heated debate, slowly empties as exhausted senators file out. Shafts of late afternoon sunlight cut through the haze, illuminating the scene of our hard-fought victory. I, Stephen Arnold Douglas, the "Little Giant" of Illinois, slump into my chair, drained but triumphant. We've done it. The Compromise of 1850 has passed, and the Union stands intact—for now.

It's been a grueling eight months since Henry Clay first introduced the omnibus bill. Poor Clay, the old compromiser, couldn't see this one through. The opposition was fierce—abolitionists and free-soilers on one side, pro-slavery hardliners on the other. But I took up the mantle, broke the bill into its component parts, and guided each piece through the legislative labyrinth. Some call it a masterstroke; others, a deal with the devil.

California enters as a free state, tipping the balance in the Senate. To appease the South, we've given them a stronger Fugitive Slave Law. New Mexico and Utah will decide the slavery question for themselves under popular sovereignty—my brainchild, my solution to this intractable problem. Let the people choose, I say. It's the most democratic way, allowing each territory to determine its own course without federal interference.

The Texas border dispute is settled, the slave trade is banned in Washington D.C., and yet slavery itself remains legal in the capital. A compromise in every sense, with something for everyone to hate.

I can already hear the criticisms. The abolitionists cry that we've capitulated to the Slave Power. The fire-eaters of the South bemoan the loss of California. And caught in the middle are men like me, trying desperately to hold this fragile Union together.

They don't understand, these ideologues on both sides. Don't they see that the alternative to compromise is disunion, even war? I've sat across the table from men like Jefferson Davis and Salmon P. Chase. I've seen the fire in their eyes, the unbending conviction. It terrifies me.

As I gather my papers and prepare to leave the chamber, I can't shake the feeling that this is but a temporary respite. The slavery question looms ever larger, threatening to tear us apart. Will popular sovereignty be enough to keep the peace? Can we continue to craft compromises as the divide grows ever wider?

I've staked my political future on this idea, this belief that democracy can solve even our most intractable problems. Perhaps this compromise will propel me toward higher office—the presidency even. But as I step out into the warm Washington night, I wonder if I've merely postponed the inevitable. The Union is preserved, yes, but for how long?

The weight of history bears down upon us all. I pray we have the strength to bear it, and that the path I've chosen today will lead our nation toward unity rather than division.

Chapter 5

A Man, Not Property

Dred Scott's Quest for Freedom, 1857

My name is Dred Scott, and I am a man, not a piece of property. Yet here I stand in 1857, the chill of a Washington winter seeping into my bones, still fighting for the freedom that should be my birthright.

I was born into slavery in Virginia, the heavy air of the tobacco fields my first memory. But my journey to freedom began when my master, Dr. Emerson, took me to live in Illinois, a free state, and then to Wisconsin Territory, where slavery was prohibited. There, I breathed the crisp air of the North, felt the soil of free land beneath my feet. There, I met and married my wife, Harriet. We have two daughters, Eliza and Lizzie. For years, we lived as free people, tasting the sweetness of liberty.

I remember a day in Wisconsin when Eliza, just learning to walk, toddled across a meadow. Harriet and I watched her, our hearts full of hope for her future. That moment of joy, of possibility, is seared into my memory.

When Dr. Emerson moved us back to Missouri, a slave state, the fetters of bondage seemed to close around us once more. But

I thought surely the time we'd spent on free soil would guarantee our freedom. I'd heard of other cases where slaves had won their freedom this way. So in 1846, with fear and hope warring in our hearts, Harriet and I filed suit for our freedom in the Missouri courts.

We lost that case, the judge's gavel striking like a physical blow. But we didn't give up. We kept fighting, through the Missouri Supreme Court, then to the federal courts, and finally, all the way to the United States Supreme Court. Each step of this legal journey has been a test of our resolve, each setback a wound to our hopes. I never imagined a simple plea for freedom could become such a momentous case, my name whispered in the halls of power.

All I want is to be recognized as a person, not property. To provide for my family as a free man. To give my daughters a chance at a better life, to see them walk across free meadows without fear. Is that so much to ask in a country that claims to value liberty above all else?

I've heard whispers of the arguments being made in Washington, each word a dagger to my heart. They say that as a black man, I'm not a citizen. That I have no right to sue in federal court. That the Constitution itself denies me the very humanity I know I possess. Each night, I hold Harriet close, whispering assurances I'm not sure I believe, watching our daughters sleep and wondering what future awaits them.

As I await the Court's decision, every day an agony of suspense, I can't help but wonder: how can a nation founded on the principle that all men are created equal still deny that simple truth to people like me? The weight of this question, of our uncertain future, presses down on me like a physical burden.

Whatever the outcome, I know that our fight for freedom won't end here. It can't. For the sake of my children, for the memory of that day in the Wisconsin meadow, and for all those still held in bondage, we must keep believing that justice will prevail. The road has been long and brutal, but we will continue to walk it, our heads held high, carrying the torch of freedom for all who would see its light.

Chapter 6

The Law of the Land

Chief Justice Taney Delivers the Dred Scott Decision, 1857

March 6, 1857

The Supreme Court chamber was tense with anticipation as I, Chief Justice Roger B. Taney, took my seat at the center of the bench. The gravity of the moment was palpable; justices, lawyers, and spectators alike seemed to hold their breath. This case, Dred Scott v. Sandford, had become more than a simple question of one man's freedom. It had evolved into a referendum on the very nature of citizenship and the future of slavery in our expanding nation.

As I prepared to deliver the Court's opinion, my mind flashed back to the heated debates that had led us to this moment. The Missouri Compromise of 1820, the Kansas-Nebraska Act, the violence in "Bleeding Kansas"—all symptoms of a nation deeply divided over the issue of slavery. This case, I knew, would either heal that divide or deepen it irreparably.

I began to read the Court's decision, my voice steady despite the weight of history pressing down upon me:

"We think they [people of African ancestry] are not, and that they are not included, and were not intended to be included, under the word 'citizens' in the Constitution, and can therefore claim none of the rights and privileges which that instrument provides for and secures to citizens of the United States."

The room seemed to collectively inhale. I continued, affirming that "The right of property in a slave is distinctly and expressly affirmed in the Constitution." With these words, we not only denied Scott his freedom but also established that Congress had no power to prohibit slavery in the territories, effectively nullifying the Missouri Compromise.

As I spoke, I could see the reactions playing out before me. Southern justices nodded in agreement, while Justices McLean and Curtis, I knew, were seething. Their dissenting opinions had been passionate and lengthy, arguing for Scott's freedom and citizenship. McLean had even gone so far as to call slavery "a blot on our national character." But the majority had spoken, and our word was final.

After the session adjourned, I retreated to my chambers, the full impact of our decision settling upon me. We had acted according to our interpretation of the Constitution, yes, but I couldn't shake the feeling that we had set in motion events beyond our control.

Would this ruling truly settle the slavery question once and for all, as I hoped? Or had we simply added fuel to an already raging fire? The Abolitionists would surely redouble their efforts now. And what of the territories? Would this decision bring peace, or would it lead to further strife as slave owners sought to expand their holdings?

As night fell over Washington, I found myself staring out the window, pondering the future of our nation. We had made our ruling based on the law as we understood it, but the law is not always just, and justice does not always bring peace.

Only time will tell the true consequences of this decision. May God grant our nation the wisdom and strength to weather whatever storms may come. For I fear that rather than settling this great question, we may have simply opened the door to an even greater conflict.

Chapter 7

A Traitor's Words

The South Reacts to Helper's Book

From the diary of Thomas Beauregard Calhoun, Charleston, South Carolina

September 15, 1857

Word has reached us of a most scandalous book published by one Hinton Rowan Helper, a North Carolinian of all people! This "Impending Crisis of the South" purports to argue against slavery on economic grounds. As if a Southerner could turn against our peculiar institution. I've sent for a copy, though I daresay it's hardly worth the paper it's printed on.

October 3, 1857

Helper's book arrived today. I must confess, it's more troubling than I anticipated. The man argues that slavery has stunted the South's economic growth, benefiting only a small planter elite while keeping the majority of whites in poverty. Preposterous!

And yet, his use of census data and economic statistics is...unse ttling. I fear this could be dangerous in the wrong hands.

November 12, 1857

The "Impending Crisis" is causing quite a stir. Abolitionists in the North are latching onto it, praising Helper as a Southern voice of reason. Reason! As if it's reasonable to advocate for the destruction of our entire way of life. Governor Adams is talking about banning the book. I'm inclined to agree—this kind of incendiary rhetoric has no place in civilized discourse.

December 20, 1857

Christmas approaches, but there's little cheer in Charleston. Helper's book has become a rallying cry for Northern Republicans. They speak of using it to appeal to non-slaveholding Southern whites. The very idea chills me to the bone. Could our yeoman farmers truly be swayed by such arguments?

January 8, 1858

A colleague at the University confided in me today that he found some of Helper's economic arguments "persuasive." I was shocked into silence. If even our educated class can be influenced by this traitorous drivel, what hope do we have? We've got to stamp this out before it spreads further.

February 17, 1858

The state legislature has officially banned "The Impending Crisis." Anyone found in possession of it can be arrested. It's an extreme measure, but necessary. Yet I fear it may be too late. The damage is done. The North has found a weapon to use against us, a Southerner's words to twist and use for their own purposes.

March 30, 1858

I lay awake at night, Helper's words echoing in my mind. "Slavery is the root of all evil in the South," he wrote. But what would we be without it? Our entire society, economy, way of life - all built on this foundation. To pull it out would be to destroy everything. And yet, the world is changing around us. I fear dark days are ahead for the South. May God preserve us from the crisis Helper predicts.

Chapter 8

The Price of Freedom

A Conductor on the Underground Railroad, 1859

Ripley, Ohio
February 12, 1859

My dear friend and fellow conductor,

I pray this letter finds you well and that our mutual friend delivers it safely. The events of the past week have left me shaken, yet more resolved than ever in our righteous cause.

Last Tuesday, as dusk fell, a rap at my door heralded the arrival of three souls seeking passage to freedom. A mother, Caroline, with her two young children, Henry and Sarah. Their eyes wild with fear, clothes tattered from their journey. They had fled from a plantation in Kentucky, evading slave catchers for near a fortnight.

Caroline's tale chilled my blood. Her husband, sold away two years past. The master's threats to sell young Sarah. The brutal beating of an elderly slave who dared to teach the children their letters. With each word, I was reminded why we must persist in this work, despite the dangers.

And dangers there are, my friend. The Fugitive Slave Act hangs over us like a executioner's ax. Since the damnable Dred Scott decision, slave catchers grow ever bolder, even here in Ohio. They burst into homes, brandishing weapons and fraudulent papers, dragging away even free blacks under the guise of "recapturing" fugitives.

We kept the family hidden in my root cellar for two days. On the second night, as we prepared for the next leg of their journey, disaster nearly struck. A patrol of slave catchers rode through town, going door to door with descriptions of Caroline and the children. My neighbor, a known sympathizer to the Southern cause, pointed them toward my home.

I've never known fear like I felt when those men pounded on my door. Caroline and the children huddled in the cellar, scarcely daring to breathe. I opened the door, heart pounding, and faced the slave catchers. By God's grace, I managed to convince them I'd seen nothing. The leader's eyes lingered on me, full of suspicion, but they moved on.

An hour later, under cover of darkness, we spirited Caroline and her children to the next station. I've not slept soundly since, starting at every sound, fearing another knock at the door.

My friend, I write not to complain of hardships, but to steel your resolve as I have steeled mine. The path we've chosen is fraught with peril, but I'm more certain than ever of its righteousness. Each soul guided to freedom is a blow struck against the monstrous institution of slavery.

Yet I fear our work grows more difficult. There's talk in Washington of strengthening the Fugitive Slave Act further. Southern fire-eaters demand more concessions, while Northern abolitionists grow more strident. I cannot shake the feeling that we're sliding toward a precipice.

But we must not falter. Not while mothers like Caroline risk all for their children's freedom. Not while the lash still falls on innocent backs. We must be the beacon of hope in this darkness.

Stay vigilant, my friend. May God grant us strength for the trials ahead.

Your faithful conductor,

Samuel Hawkins

P.S. Burn this letter after reading. We cannot be too careful.

Chapter 9

Fire in the Night

John Brown's Raid on Harpers Ferry, 1859

Urgent Report to Colonel Robert E. Lee
From: Sergeant Thomas Jeffords, Virginia Militia
Date: October 18, 1859

Colonel Lee,

I write this report with a hand still shaking from the events of the past two days. What transpired here in Harpers Ferry beggars belief, yet I swear every word to be true.

On the night of October 16, our quiet town erupted into chaos. A band of armed men, led by the infamous abolitionist John Brown, seized the federal armory. Their aim, as we later discovered, was to incite a slave rebellion and bring the war against slavery to Southern soil.

The initial attack caught us completely unawares. Brown and his men, numbering about 20, including several Negroes, over-whelmed the armory's watchman with ease. They then proceeded to cut the telegraph wires and seize hostages from prominent local families.

The first we knew of the attack was when a free Negro man came running into town, shouting that "men were killing people at the armory." I rallied what men I could, but in the darkness and confusion, it was hard to discern friend from foe.

What followed was a night of terror and bewilderment. Shots rang out sporadically. Hostages cried out from the armory. And all the while, we feared that at any moment, the local slaves might rise up to join Brown's men.

By dawn, we had the armory surrounded, but Brown's men were well-fortified. They exchanged fire with us throughout the day. I saw good men fall, Colonel. Their blood cries out for justice.

Most puzzling was the behavior of the local slaves. Despite Brown's calls for them to join his "army of emancipation," they remained largely indifferent. Some even aided in the defense of their masters' homes. It seems Brown's grand vision of slave insurrection was little more than a madman's fantasy.

The tide turned with the arrival of a detachment of U.S. Marines under your command, Colonel. Their assault on the armory's engine house, where Brown and his remaining men had barricaded themselves with hostages, was swift and decisive.

I watched as Brown was dragged out, bloodied but alive. His face, Colonel, I'll not soon forget. There was no remorse there, no fear. Only a zealot's unyielding conviction.

In the aftermath, we've discovered disturbing evidence of broader support for Brown's raid. Northern-made weapons, maps of the region, and documents suggesting a network of sympathizers. Colonel, I fear this is but a harbinger of worse to come.

The raid is over, but its echoes will long resonate. Already, I hear whispers of secession, of war. Southern blood has been spilled by Northern abolitionists. How can this breach be healed?

I await your further orders, Colonel. But I urge you, please impress upon Richmond and Washington the gravity of what has transpired here. John Brown may hang, but I fear his spirit will long haunt us.

Your obedient servant,

Sergeant Thomas Jeffords

Chapter 10

The Springfield Gazette Announces: Lincoln Elected President, Nov. 1860

THE SPRINGFIELD GAZETTE
November 7, 1860

ABRAHAM LINCOLN ELECTED 16TH PRESIDENT OF THE UNITED STATES

SPRINGFIELD, ILLINOIS - In a stunning turn of events that has sent shockwaves through the nation, our own Abraham Lincoln has been elected as the 16th President of the United States. The tall, lanky lawyer from Illinois, known for his honest character and staunch opposition to the expansion of slavery, has secured victory in one of the most contentious elections in our nation's history.

ELECTORAL COLLEGE FAVORS LINCOLN

While final vote tallies are still being calculated, it is clear that Mr. Lincoln has secured a majority in the Electoral College, guaranteeing his ascension to the highest office in the land. Current projections show Lincoln winning 180 electoral votes, well above the 152 needed for victory.

POPULAR VOTE SPLIT AMONG FOUR CANDIDATES

However, our readers should note that Mr. Lincoln's victory comes without a majority of the popular vote. In an unusual four-way race, the Republican standard-bearer appears to have won only about 40% of the popular vote. The preliminary results are as follows:

- Abraham Lincoln (Republican): 40%

- Stephen Douglas (Northern Democrat): 29%

- John C. Breckinridge (Southern Democrat): 18%

- John Bell (Constitutional Union): 13%

This split in the Democratic Party, with Northern and Southern factions running separate candidates, undoubtedly contributed to Mr. Lincoln's success.

SOUTHERN STATES REJECT LINCOLN

It is worth noting that Mr. Lincoln's name did not even appear on the ballot in ten Southern states. His support came almost entirely from the North and West, raising concerns about how his presidency will be received in the South.

REACTION AND CONCERNS

While celebrations have erupted here in Springfield and across much of the North, reports from the South indicate a much grimmer mood. There is already talk in some quarters of secession, though it remains to be seen whether such drastic action will be taken.

Mr. Lincoln has consistently stated that he has no intention of interfering with slavery where it already exists, but his opposition to its expansion into new territories has made him a controversial figure in the South.

As we look toward Mr. Lincoln's inauguration in March, the nation holds its breath. Will our new President be able to hold the Union together in the face of such division? Only time will tell.

The Springfield Gazette will continue to bring you updates as this momentous story unfolds.

Chapter II

A New Nation Born

The Founding of the Confederate States of America, 1861

Montgomery, Alabama - February 8, 1861

Speech by William Lowndes Yancey, Alabama delegate:

"Gentlemen of the Convention, we stand here today having accomplished what our forefathers did nearly a century ago. We have cast off the yoke of a tyrannical government and forged a new nation, conceived in liberty and dedicated to the proposition that our rights and our property shall not be infringed upon by those who do not understand our way of life.

"In this past week, we have achieved what many thought impossible. We have united seven sovereign states—South Carolina, Mississippi, Florida, Alabama, Georgia, Louisiana, and Texas—into a new confederation. We have drafted and adopted a constitution that protects our interests and upholds the principles for which we have long fought.

"Our constitution affirms the right of property in slaves, a right denied and threatened by the government in Washington. It ensures that no law denying or impairing the right of property in negro slaves shall be passed. We have guaranteed the rights of our states to govern themselves without interference from a central authority that does not represent our interests.

"Let it be known that we did not take this action lightly. For years, we have watched as the North has grown increasingly hostile to our institutions, our property, and our very way of life. The election of Abraham Lincoln, a man who would not even appear on our ballots, was the final stroke. We could not and would not submit to a government dominated by those who would destroy us.

"And now, we have selected a leader to guide us through these perilous times. A man of principle, of courage, and of deep understanding of the Southern cause. I speak, of course, of Jefferson Davis of Mississippi, whom we have elected as the first President of the Confederate States of America."

As William Lowndes Yancey concluded his rousing speech, a tall, lean man with piercing blue eyes and a rigid posture made his way to the podium. Jefferson Davis, recently a U.S. Senator from Mississippi, now stood before the convention as the chosen leader of a new nation. The weight of the moment was visible in the deep lines of his face and the slight tremor in his hand as he gripped the podium.

Davis paused, his gaze sweeping across the assembled delegates. Many knew him as a fierce defender of Southern rights, a Mexican War hero, and a former U.S. Secretary of War. But today, he was to assume a mantle he had never sought nor desired.

Taking a deep breath, Davis began his inaugural address:

"Fellow citizens and compatriots of the Confederate States of America, I stand before you today humbled by the task ahead and grateful for the trust you have placed in me."

As he spoke, Davis's voice grew stronger, his words infused with the conviction of a man who had spent a lifetime preparing for this moment, though he had never known it. He touched on his personal experience as a planter, a soldier, and a statesman, drawing parallels between his own journey and that of the new nation he was to lead.

"Like many of you," he said, his voice tinged with emotion, "I have known the joy of seeing a crop flourish under the Southern sun, worked by hands that have known no other way of life. I have felt the sting of Northern contempt for our traditions and our rights. And I have witnessed, in the halls of Congress, the slow erosion of the principles upon which this great experiment in democracy was founded."

Davis's words resonated with the audience, many of whom nodded in agreement. They saw in him not just a president, but an embodiment of their cause—a Southern gentleman, a skilled orator, and a staunch defender of their way of life.

As he concluded his speech, Davis's voice softened, becoming almost paternal in its tone. "We embark today on a path fraught with peril, but guided by the righteousness of our cause. Let us go forward from this day with courage and determination, secure in the knowledge that our new nation is founded on the soundest of principles."

With these words, Jefferson Davis, the reluctant rebel turned president, set the Confederate States of America on its course towards independence - and war.

1861

Chapter 12

The First Shot

General Beauregard and the Battle of Fort Sumter, April 1861

Charleston, South Carolina - April 14, 1861

The acrid smell of gunpowder still hangs in the air as I, General Pierre Gustave Toutant Beauregard, survey the battered walls of Fort Sumter. The events of the past few days weigh heavily on my mind. I have just witnessed – nay, orchestrated – the opening salvo of what may become a great and terrible war.

It was but a few days ago, on April 10th, that I received word from the Confederate government in Montgomery to demand the evacuation of Fort Sumter. Major Robert Anderson and his Union garrison had become a thorn in our side, a symbol of Northern authority in the heart of our new nation.

I sent my aides to the fort with an offer of surrender. I confess, a part of me hoped Anderson would see reason. After all, he had been my artillery instructor at West Point. But Anderson, ever the soldier, refused to abandon his post without orders from his government.

Left with no choice, I gave the order to open fire in the early hours of April 12th. The boom of the first shot echoed across Charleston Harbor at 4:30 a.m., fired from Fort Johnson. Soon, batteries from all around the harbor joined in the bombardment.

For 34 hours, we rained fire upon Fort Sumter. The sight was both terrible and magnificent—shells arcing through the air, explosions lighting up the night sky. Through it all, Anderson and his men held firm, returning fire as best they could with their limited armaments.

It wasn't until the afternoon of April 13th that Anderson finally agreed to evacuate. The fort was in ruins, its wooden structures ablaze from our hot shot. The men were exhausted, their supplies nearly depleted. They had fought bravely, but the outcome was never in doubt.

Now, as I watch the Stars and Stripes lowered and our Confederate flag raised over the battered ramparts, I am struck by a curious fact: despite the ferocity of our bombardment, not a single soldier on either side was killed in the battle. It seems almost miraculous, a small mercy in what I fear may become a bloodbath.

The Union troops departed with dignity, allowed to salute their flag and take their personal property. As they sailed away, I couldn't help but wonder: how many more forts will fall? How many of my former comrades will I face across the field of battle?

We have won this first engagement, but at what cost? The North will surely retaliate. President Lincoln will have no choice but to call for troops, to attempt to subdue what he sees as a rebellion. But we are no mere rebels—we are a new nation, fighting for our independence, our way of life.

As night falls over Charleston, I pen my report to the government in Montgomery. "Fort Sumter is ours," I write, the words seeming inadequate to capture the magnitude of what has transpired. The first shot has been fired. There is no turning back now.

Chapter 13

A Terrible Resolve

Lincoln's Response to Fort Sumter, April 1861

Washington, D.C. - April 15, 1861

The weight of the nation presses down upon me as I sit alone in my office, the events of the past days echoing through my mind. Fort Sumter has fallen. The unthinkable has happened—Americans have fired upon Americans. The rebellion I had hoped to avoid has begun in earnest.

I, Abraham Lincoln, 16th President of these United States, now face the gravest decision of my life. The bombardment of Fort Sumter cannot go unanswered. To do nothing would be to acquiesce to the dissolution of our Union, to betray the oath I swore to preserve, protect, and defend the Constitution.

Major Anderson and his men fought bravely, holding out for 34 hours against overwhelming odds. By the grace of God, no lives were lost in the battle. But I fear this is only the beginning. The blood of patriots and rebels alike will soon stain this land if I cannot find a way to swiftly end this insurrection.

I've spent the night in consultation with my cabinet and military advisors. Their counsel weighs heavily upon me, as does the realization that my next actions may plunge this nation into full-scale civil war. Yet, what choice do I have? Seven states have already seceded, and others teeter on the brink. I cannot allow this rebellion to spread further.

The Constitution grants me the power to call forth the militia to suppress insurrections. It is a power I had hoped never to use, but the time for hope has passed. Action is now required.

I have drafted a proclamation calling for 75,000 volunteers to serve for three months. It seems a large number, but my military advisors assure me it will be sufficient to put down this rebellion quickly. I pray they are right.

In this proclamation, I will also call for a special session of Congress on July 4th. It seems fitting to reconvene our government on the anniversary of our independence, as we fight to preserve the Union our forefathers established.

As I put pen to paper, I am acutely aware of the magnitude of this moment. With these words, I will be committing our nation to a course from which there may be no turning back. Families will be torn apart, brothers may face each other on the battlefield, and blood will be shed on American soil.

Yet, I see no other path. The Union must be preserved. The Constitution must be upheld. And this rebellion must be put down, swiftly and decisively.

May God grant us the wisdom and strength for the trials ahead, and may He have mercy on our divided nation.

Chapter 14

A Tale of Two Citizens

Early War Reflections, June 1861

Boston, Massachusetts - June 15, 1861

Elias Merriweather wiped the sweat from his brow as he re-stocked shelves in his general store. The summer heat was oppressive, but not nearly as suffocating as the worry that had settled over him these past months.

"Another shipment delayed," he muttered, reviewing his ledger. The war was barely two months old, and already it was wreaking havoc on his business. But that was the least of his concerns.

His son Thomas had been talking about enlisting ever since Lincoln's call for volunteers. Sarah, his wife, was beside herself with worry. "It'll be over by Christmas," Elias had assured her, but doubt gnawed at him.

As he closed up shop, a group of young men marched by, singing patriotic songs. Their enthusiasm both heartened and troubled him. Did they truly understand what they were marching into?

Later that evening, as his family sat down to dinner, Elias cleared his throat. "I've been thinking," he began cautiously, "perhaps I should enlist myself."

The clatter of dropped silverware punctuated the sudden silence. Sarah's eyes widened in shock, while Thomas leaned forward eagerly.

"But Pa," his daughter Emily protested, "you're too old!"

Elias chuckled despite himself. "I'm only 42, Emily. Plenty of men my age are joining up."

As the family debated late into the night, Elias found his resolve strengthening. This rebellion had to be put down quickly, for the good of the nation. And if that meant leaving his store and family behind for a spell, so be it.

Still, as he lay in bed that night, images of the South he'd visited years ago flashed through his mind. How had it come to this? Americans fighting Americans? He prayed for a swift end to the conflict, even as a nagging voice whispered that this war might be longer and bloodier than anyone imagined.

****

Outside Atlanta, Georgia - June 18, 1861

Jeremiah Calhoun squinted against the setting sun as he surveyed his cotton fields. The crop looked good this year, but who would buy it with the Yankees blockading Southern ports?

He spat on the ground, a mixture of tobacco juice and contempt. "Damn Yankees," he muttered. "Can't leave us be to live as we please."

As he walked back to the house, Jeremiah's mind wandered to his eldest son, William, who had joined the 8th Georgia Infantry. The boy had marched off full of fire and vinegar, talking about whipping ten Yankees before breakfast. Jeremiah prayed his son's confidence wasn't misplaced.

Inside, he found Mary mending uniforms for the local militia. She looked up as he entered, concern etching her features. "Any news?"

Jeremiah shook his head. "Nothing yet. But I reckon we'll be hearing about a big battle soon enough. Our boys won't let them take Virginia without a fight."

As they sat down to a simple supper, James, his younger son, could barely contain his excitement. "Pa, when can I join up? I'm near as tall as Will now!"

Jeremiah fixed his son with a stern look. "You're needed here, boy. Someone's got to help me bring in the harvest."

In truth, Jeremiah was grateful for any excuse to keep James home a while longer. One son in harm's way was enough.

Later, as crickets chirped in the warm Georgia night, Jeremiah sat on the porch, cleaning his old hunting rifle. The war still felt distant, but he couldn't shake the feeling that it would reach them soon enough.

"We didn't want this war," he mused aloud, "but by God, we'll finish it. The North will learn they can't trample on our rights and way of life."

Yet, as he gazed up at the stars, a flicker of doubt crossed his mind. The Union had more men, more factories, more ships. Could Southern courage and determination overcome such odds?

Pushing the thought aside, Jeremiah stood and headed to bed. Whatever came, he and his kin would face it head-on. That's what Southerners did.

Chapter 15

Shattered Illusions

Lincoln Learns of Bull Run, July 1861

Washington D.C. - July 22, 1861

The somber atmosphere in the White House study matched the grim expression on Simon Cameron's face as he entered. President Abraham Lincoln looked up from his desk, instantly alert at the sight of his Secretary of War.

"Mr. President," Cameron began, his voice heavy, "I have news from Manassas Junction. It's...not good, sir."

Lincoln gestured for Cameron to sit. "Tell me everything, Simon. Don't spare the details."

Cameron sank into the chair, his shoulders slumped. "Our forces under General McDowell engaged the rebels yesterday at Bull Run. Initial reports were promising. We pushed them back, and victory seemed within our grasp."

"But?" Lincoln prompted, sensing the turn in the narrative.

"But the Confederate reinforcements arrived—Johnston's army from the Shenandoah and Beauregard's men. They rallied and counterattacked. Our lines broke, sir. The retreat...it turned into a rout."

Lincoln's eyes widened. "A rout? Our boys just ran?"

Cameron nodded grimly. "I'm afraid so, Mr. President. The road back to Washington was choked with fleeing soldiers, congressmen who'd come to watch the battle, and civilian picnickers. It was chaos."

"Good God," Lincoln muttered. "Casualties?"

"Still coming in, but early reports suggest around 3,000 killed, wounded, or missing on our side. The Confederates suffered too, but they hold the field."

Lincoln stood, pacing the room. "And what of our army now?"

"Scattered, demoralized. McDowell's trying to regroup and establish defensive positions, but..." Cameron trailed off.

"But the dream of a quick, decisive victory has vanished," Lincoln finished.

"Yes, sir. I'm afraid this war may be longer and bloodier than any of us anticipated."

Lincoln stopped at the window, gazing out at the city. After a long moment, he turned back to Cameron. "What's your assessment of McDowell's leadership in this affair?"

Cameron shifted uncomfortably. "He had a sound plan, sir, but its execution...Perhaps a more experienced commander might have..."

"Might have what?" Lincoln interrupted. "Held the line? Prevented the rout? Or are we simply unprepared for the realities of this war?"

"It's possible we need a change in command, Mr. President. Someone with more..." Cameron searched for the right word.

"Someone with more fire," Lincoln mused. "Someone who can shape these volunteers into a real fighting force."

"There's talk of General McClellan," Cameron ventured. "He's had success in Western Virginia."

Lincoln nodded slowly. "Perhaps. We'll need to consider our options carefully. This defeat changes everything, Simon. The rebels will be emboldened. Our people will be shaken. We must act decisively."

As Cameron stood to leave, Lincoln added, "And Simon? We'll need more men. Many more. This war has only just begun." As he spoke, Lincoln's brow furrowed deeply, the lines etching themselves more prominently into his already careworn face.

After the Secretary of War had gone, Lincoln slumped in his chair, the weight of the presidency bearing down on him like never before. The cheery predictions of a 90-day war lay shattered, and the long, bloody struggle he had feared loomed ahead.

"Oh, if I had known what a terrible thing I was getting into," he murmured to the empty room. Lincoln stood slowly, feeling as if he had aged years in the span of this single conversation. He moved to the window, gazing out at the city that had so recently buzzed with excitement for the coming battle. Now, an eerie quiet seemed to have settled over Washington.

"A house divided against itself cannot stand," Lincoln whispered, recalling his own words from what now felt like a lifetime ago. "I said we would become all one thing, or all the other. But at what cost?" He closed his eyes, steeling himself for the difficult days ahead. The fate of the Union now rested squarely on his shoulders, and he felt the full weight of that burden.

Chapter 16

Victory's Aftermath

Lee Briefs Davis on Bull Run, July 1861

Richmond, Virginia - July 22, 1861

President Jefferson Davis sat behind his desk, his lean face etched with a mixture of relief and concern. The flickering lamplight cast shadows across his sharp features, accentuating the weariness in his eyes. Across from him stood Colonel Robert E. Lee, his military advisor, ramrod straight despite the late hour. Lee's greying hair and dignified bearing gave him an air of quiet authority, a stark contrast to the nervous energy that seemed to fill the room.

"Well, Robert," Davis began, "it seems congratulations are in order. But I'd like your full assessment of the situation."

Lee nodded, his manner calm and composed. "Mr. President, our forces under Generals Beauregard and Johnston have indeed achieved a significant victory at Manassas Junction. The Federal army has been routed and driven back to Washington."

Davis leaned forward, his eyes sharp. "And the details of the engagement?"

"The battle began yesterday morning," Lee explained. "Initially, the Federal forces under McDowell had the upper hand. They pushed our troops back along Bull Run. However, the arrival of Johnston's army from the Shenandoah Valley turned the tide."

"Ah, yes," Davis interjected. "Johnston's timely arrival. We must commend the railroad for that swift transport."

Lee continued, "Indeed, sir. But there's another factor I must bring to your attention. A brigade commander, Brigadier General Thomas J. Jackson, played a crucial role in holding our line."

Davis raised an eyebrow. "Jackson? I'm not familiar with him."

"He's a Virginia Military Institute professor, sir. During the heat of the battle, when our lines were wavering, he held his ground with his brigade. Brigadier General Barnard Bee, while trying to rally his own troops, was heard shouting, 'There stands Jackson like a stone wall! Rally behind the Virginians!'"

Lee's voice softened slightly. "Unfortunately, General Bee was mortally wounded shortly after, but his words about Jackson seem to have left an impression."

A small smile played on Davis's lips. "Stonewall Jackson, is it? We'll have to keep an eye on him."

Lee nodded in agreement before continuing, "The Federal retreat quickly turned into a rout. The road back to Washington was clogged with fleeing soldiers and even civilians who had come to watch the battle."

"Civilians?" Davis's voice held a note of disbelief.

"Yes, sir. It seems many in Washington expected this to be a quick, decisive battle. A spectacle, even." Lee's voice took on a hint of disdain. "They came in carriages, with picnic baskets, as if to a summer outing. Some even brought opera glasses to better view the 'show.' The battle's reality must have come as a terrible shock."

Davis shook his head. "They'll know better now. What of our losses?"

Lee's face grew somber, a flicker of pain crossing his features. "Substantial, Mr. President. Early reports suggest around 2,000 casualties on our side. The Federal losses are likely higher." He paused, his voice softening. "It's a strange thing, sir, to celebrate a victory knowing that many of the men lying dead on that field once called me their commander. This war will test not just our strength, but our hearts as well."

A heavy silence fell over the room. After a moment, Davis spoke, "And what do you make of this victory, Robert? Should we press our advantage? March on Washington?"

Lee considered carefully before responding. "Sir, while the victory is significant, our army is also disorganized after the battle. Many of our troops are as green as the Federals. I would caution against overextending ourselves."

Davis nodded slowly. "Ever the voice of prudence, Robert. But surely we must capitalize on this victory somehow."

"Indeed, Mr. President. I believe this battle has bought us valuable time. Time to train our forces, to strengthen our defenses. The Yankees will not take us lightly again."

As Lee finished his report, Davis stood and walked to the window, gazing out at the Richmond night. "Very well, Robert. We'll consolidate our gains for now. But mark my words, this is only the beginning. The Yankees may have greater numbers and resources, but we have the righteous cause and the indomitable spirit of our people."

He turned back to Lee, his eyes glinting with determination. "We'll make them understand that we won't be subjugated. Whatever the cost, we'll defend our rights and our way of life."

Lee nodded solemnly. "Yes, Mr. President. May God be with us in the trials ahead." As he turned to leave, Lee's gaze fell on a map of Virginia on Davis's wall. For a moment, he allowed himself to feel the full weight of what lay ahead—a war against the very nation he had served for decades, against men he had once called brothers in arms. With a barely perceptible sigh, he straightened his shoulders and strode out, ready to face whatever challenges the coming days would bring.

Chapter 17

The Young Napoleon

McClellan Takes Command, November 1861

In the wake of the disastrous defeat at Bull Run, President Lincoln sought a leader who could restore confidence and whip the Union Army into fighting shape. His eyes turned to Major General George B. McClellan, a 34-year-old West Point graduate who had achieved early successes in Western Virginia.

McClellan, nicknamed "The Young Napoleon" for his strategic mind and ambition, was appointed commander of the Army of the Potomac on July 26, 1861. Impressed by McClellan's organizational skills and the army's improving morale, Lincoln took the next step. On November 1, 1861, he appointed McClellan general-in-chief of all Union armies, replacing the aging Winfield Scott.

As McClellan settled into his new, expanded role, he began to outline his vision for the entire war effort...

****

November 5, 1861 - Washington, D.C.

General George B. McClellan's Personal Notes:

The task before me is monumental, but I am confident in my ability to see it through. President Lincoln has placed his trust in me, and I shall not disappoint him or this great nation.

First and foremost, we must transform this rabble into a proper army. The defeat at Bull Run has made it painfully clear that enthusiasm alone is not enough. We need discipline, training, and organization.

Key points to address:

1. Training: Implement a rigorous training regimen. These volunteers must learn to move, fight, and follow orders like professional soldiers. Drill, drill, and more drill.

2. Organization: Restructure the army into corps, divisions, and brigades. Clear chain of command is essential.

3. Supply and Logistics: Ensure our men are well-equipped and supplied. No more scandals of shoddy uniforms or defective weapons.

4. Fortifications: Washington must be made impregnable. I will not risk the capital falling into rebel hands.

5. Intelligence: Expand and improve our intelligence-gathering capabilities. We must know the enemy's strength and movements.

6. Strategy: Develop a comprehensive strategy for victory. My thoughts lean towards a grand flanking movement, perhaps utilizing the Navy to outmaneuver the rebels.

I must be cautious, however. Rush into battle unprepared, and we risk another Bull Run. The men need time to train, to become a true fighting force. Lincoln and his cabinet may grow impatient, but I must stand firm. Better to take the time to build an overwhelming force than to risk defeat through haste.

The rebel armies are not to be underestimated. Their generals - Lee, Johnston, Beauregard - are skilled. But I have studied war all my life. I know how to defeat them.

My greatest concern is political interference. Already I sense the meddling hands of Congress and the Cabinet. They must understand that this is a military matter, to be handled by military men. I alone should dictate the army's movements and timing.

I feel the weight of history upon my shoulders. The fate of the Union rests in my hands. But I am ready for this challenge. With proper preparation and execution of my plans, we shall crush this rebellion and restore the Union.

The road ahead will be long and difficult, but I have no doubt of our ultimate victory. I will give this nation the army it needs and the leadership it deserves.

God grant me the strength and wisdom for the task ahead.

G.B. McClellan
Maj. Gen., Commanding

Chapter 18

Anaconda's Squeeze

A Moral Quandary in Our Naval Strategy, November 1861

The Boston Herald
November 15, 1861
By Edwin Aldridge, Special Correspondent

As our nation finds itself embroiled in an increasingly bitter civil conflict, we must pause to consider the methods by which we wage this war. Today, I wish to draw the reader's attention to the Union's naval blockade of Southern ports, the so-called "Anaconda Plan," and its impact not on the Confederate war machine, but on the common people of the South.

Implemented by presidential proclamation on April 19th of this year, this blockade stretches over 3,500 miles of coastline from Virginia to Texas. Its aim, as explained by former General-in-Chief Winfield Scott, is to strangle the Confederacy's economy and war effort by cutting off trade with Europe and denying the rebels access to vital supplies.

On paper, it is a sound strategy. Indeed, reports suggest that cotton exports from the South have already dropped dramatically, from 3.8 million bales last year to a projected 1.5 million bales this year. Naval patrols have captured or turned back dozens of ships attempting to run the blockade.

Yet, as we congratulate ourselves on this tactical success, we must ask: at what cost do we achieve it?

Recent accounts from Southern port cities paint a grim picture. In Charleston, Mobile, and New Orleans, prices for common goods have skyrocketed. Coffee, once a staple on every breakfast table, now sells for $5 a pound when available at all. Sugar, salt, and manufactured goods grow scarce. Medicines, many of which were imported from Europe, are in desperately short supply.

It is not the wealthy planters or Confederate officials who suffer most from these shortages. It is the common folk—the shop-keepers, laborers, and small farmers. It is the wives struggling to feed their children, the elderly deprived of needed medicines, the workers facing unemployment as Southern ports grow quiet.

One must wonder: Is this the way to reunite our sundered nation? By inflicting hardship on those least responsible for this rebellion?

Proponents of the blockade argue that it is a necessary evil, a bloodless way to shorten the war and ultimately save lives. They contend that by strangling the South's economy, we force the Confederacy to the negotiating table. Yet, history teaches us that such tactics often backfire, hardening resolve rather than breaking it.

Consider the British blockade of France during the Napoleonic Wars. Did it bring France to its knees? No, it merely fueled resentment and nationalism among the French people. Are we not risking the same with our Southern brethren?

Moreover, we must question the long-term consequences of such a strategy. Even if successful in military terms, what then? Do we expect to re-integrate a resentful, economically ruined South back into the Union? How many years – nay, decades – would it take to rebuild not just the Southern economy, but the trust and goodwill necessary for a truly united nation?

Some might argue that the civilians of the South, by not actively opposing secession, bear some responsibility for this conflict. But let us be honest with ourselves—how many of us in the North have the courage to openly defy our government, even when we disagree with its policies? Can we rightfully expect more from Southern civilians?

Perhaps there is a middle ground. Could we not modify the blockade to allow humanitarian supplies – food, medicine, and other necessities – while still restricting military goods? Could we not target the blockade more precisely at known military supply routes, rather than indiscriminately choking all Southern ports?

Or perhaps we should reconsider our entire approach to this war. Instead of a strategy of economic strangulation, could we not focus our efforts on decisive military engagements, as in General McClellan's proposed Peninsula Campaign? Might this not bring a swifter end to the conflict with less collateral damage to civilian lives?

As we ponder these questions, let us remember the words of our beloved President Lincoln in his recent inaugural address: "We are not enemies, but friends. We must not be enemies." If we truly believe these words, then we must carefully consider whether our current strategy aligns with our ultimate goal—not just victory, but reconciliation.

The Anaconda Plan may well strangle the Confederacy, but at what cost to our national soul? As citizens of this great republic, we must demand that our military and political leaders consider not just the expediency of their tactics, but their moral implications as well.

For if we win this war but lose our humanity in the process, can we truly call it a victory?

Chapter 19

A Diplomat's Gambit

John Slidell Recalls the Trent Affair

From the Memoirs of John Slidell, Written in 1868

As I sit here in Paris, my adopted home these past years, my mind often wanders back to that fateful November day in 1861. At the ripe age of 75, I can now look back on the Trent Affair with a mixture of amusement and frustration. How close we came to changing the course of the war, and yet how spectacularly it all unraveled.

It was a crisp autumn morning when James Mason and I, along with our secretaries, boarded the British mail packet RMS Trent in Havana. Our mission was clear: as newly appointed envoys of the Confederate States of America, we were to sail to Europe to seek recognition and support for our cause. I was bound for France, Mason for England.

We knew, of course, that our journey was fraught with danger. The Yankees' blockade was in full effect, and we had already eluded their patrols once by slipping out of Charleston under cover of darkness. But once aboard the Trent, flying the Union Jack, we felt a sense of security. After all, would the Union dare to interfere with a British vessel?

How naive we were.

On November 8th, barely a day out of Havana, our world was thrown into chaos. The USS San Jacinto, commanded by Captain Charles Wilkes, intercepted the Trent in the Bahama Channel. I'll never forget the boom of their cannon, firing across our bow. Before we knew it, Union sailors were boarding our ship, brandishing weapons and demanding our surrender.

Captain Wilkes, acting without orders from Washington, had taken it upon himself to capture us. The British captain of the Trent protested vehemently, but to no avail. Mason and I were forcibly removed from the ship, along with our secretaries.

As we were taken aboard the San Jacinto, I remember thinking that Wilkes had just handed the Confederacy a golden opportunity. Surely, I thought, this blatant violation of British neutrality would force Her Majesty's government to recognize the Confederacy and enter the war on our side.

The weeks that followed were a whirlwind. We were imprisoned at Fort Warren in Boston Harbor, while across the Atlantic, tensions between Britain and the Union reached a fever pitch. The British, their pride wounded and their neutrality violated, demanded our release and began preparing for war.

For a brief, shining moment, it seemed our capture might accomplish more than our mission ever could. The Confederacy waited with bated breath for Britain to declare war on the Union.

But it was not to be. Lincoln and his Secretary of State, Seward, proved craftier than we had given them credit for. They released Mason and me, claiming Wilkes had acted without authority, and offered an apology to the British. Just like that, the crisis was defused.

On January 1, 1862, we were finally released and allowed to continue our journey to Europe. But the moment had passed. Britain, satisfied with the Union's apology, remained neutral. Our mission, though we pursued it for years, never achieved its primary goal of gaining European recognition for the Confederacy.

Now, looking back after all these years, I can't help but wonder how differently the war might have unfolded had Britain entered the fray. Would the Confederacy have achieved its independence? Would I be penning these memoirs from Richmond rather than Paris?

Such speculations are the luxury of old age, I suppose. The Trent Affair, for all its sound and fury, ultimately changed little. But it serves as a stark reminder of how seemingly small incidents can bring great nations to the brink of war—and how skilled diplomacy can pull them back again.

Chapter 20

A Wartime Christmas

Elias and Jeremiah, December 1861

Boston, Massachusetts - December 24, 1861

The Merriweather home was festooned with evergreen boughs and red ribbons, but the Christmas cheer felt forced this year. Elias stood by the fireplace, warming his hands and watching his family.

Sarah busied herself arranging treats on a platter, her movements quick and nervous. Thomas, home on leave from his training camp, sat in uniform, looking older than his 18 years. Emily hung the last ornament on the tree, her usual excitement subdued.

"Well," Elias said, breaking the silence, "shall we sing some carols?"

Before anyone could respond, a knock at the door startled them all. Thomas tensed visibly.

Elias opened the door to find his neighbor, Mrs. Abernathy, clutching a small package. "For Thomas," she said, her eyes glistening. "My John wanted him to have it." Her son had fallen at Ball's Bluff just two months ago.

As Elias rejoined his family, Sarah asked softly, "What did she want?"

"A gift for Thomas," he replied, handing over the package. "From John Abernathy."

The room fell silent as Thomas unwrapped a pair of warm wool socks and a letter. He read it quietly, then folded it carefully and put it in his pocket.

"Thank you for letting me enlist, Pa," Thomas said, his voice thick with emotion.

Elias nodded, unable to speak. He'd resisted at first, but after Bull Run, it seemed everyone was joining up.

As they gathered around the piano to sing, Elias couldn't shake a feeling of foreboding. Would this be their last Christmas together? He pushed the thought aside and joined in the first wavering notes of "Silent Night."

****

Outside Atlanta, Georgia - December 25, 1861

The Calhoun farm was quieter than usual this Christmas. Jeremiah sat on the porch, whittling a small wooden horse as he watched the sun set on an unusually warm December day.

Inside, he could hear Mary humming as she prepared their modest Christmas supper. The scent of cornbread and ham wafted out to him. James and Rebecca were setting the table, their chatter a poor substitute for the boisterous family gatherings of years past.

"Pa!" James called from inside. "Letter from Will!"

Jeremiah's heart leapt. He hurried inside, taking the precious envelope from James. The family gathered around as he read aloud:

"Dear Ma, Pa, James, and Becca,

Merry Christmas from Virginia! Don't you fret about me. We've got plenty of food and warm clothes thanks to the ladies' aid societies. Tell Ma her socks are the envy of my whole company.

I miss you all something fierce, but I'm proud to be defending our home and rights. We'll lick these Yankees come spring, just you wait and see.

Your loving son and brother,

William"

Mary wiped a tear from her eye. "At least he's safe and warm," she said softly.

Jeremiah nodded, folding the letter carefully. "That's our boy," he said gruffly, hiding his own emotion.

As they sat down to supper, Jeremiah looked at the empty chair where William should have been. "Let us pray," he said, taking Mary's hand. "Lord, we thank you for this food and for keeping our William safe. We pray for a swift end to this war and the safe return of all our boys. Amen."

"Amen," the family echoed.

As they ate, Jeremiah tried to keep the conversation cheerful, but the war hung over them like a shadow. The blockade had made coffee and sugar scarce, and he worried about getting enough seed for next year's planting.

Still, as he looked at his family's faces in the candlelight, Jeremiah felt a surge of determination. Whatever hardships lay ahead, they would face them together. This was what they were fighting for.

1862

Chapter 21

Ironclads and Empires

The Admiralty Grapples with a New Age, March 1862

As the American Civil War raged on, its impact reached far beyond the shores of the United States. The Battle of Hampton Roads, featuring the first clash between ironclad warships, sent shockwaves through naval circles worldwide. Nowhere was this felt more keenly than in Great Britain, whose wooden fleet had long dominated the seas. The following confidential correspondence reveals how the world's preeminent naval power grappled with this revolutionary development.

****

CONFIDENTIAL

To: First Lord of the Admiralty, The Duke of Somerset
From: Captain Sir Alexander Milne, North America and West
   Indies Station

Date: 15 March 1862

My Lord,

I write to you with a matter of utmost urgency concerning recent events in the waters off Hampton Roads, Virginia. Our naval attaché in Washington has forwarded a series of reports detailing a naval engagement of unprecedented nature between ironclad vessels of the United States Navy and the Confederate States Navy.

On March 8th, the Confederate ironclad CSS Virginia (formerly USS Merrimack) engaged wooden warships of the Union fleet. The results were nothing short of catastrophic for the wooden vessels. The Virginia destroyed the USS Cumberland and Congress with minimal damage to herself, demonstrating a devastating superiority over traditional warships.

However, on March 9th, the United States' own ironclad, USS Monitor, arrived and engaged the Virginia. What followed was a battle that, I do not exaggerate, my Lord, will revolutionize naval warfare as we know it.

Enclosed you will find detailed reports from our attaché and several eyewitness accounts we've managed to procure. I draw your attention specifically to the following points:

1. Both ironclads proved virtually impervious to the other's cannon fire. The engagement lasted several hours with neither able to decisively defeat the other.

2. The Monitor's rotating turret design allowed it to fire in multiple directions without maneuvering the entire ship, a significant tactical advantage.

3. The low profile of the Monitor made it a difficult target, while its shallow draft allowed it to maneuver in waters where deeper-drafted vessels could not go.

4. Despite the Virginia's size advantage, the Monitor's superior maneuverability negated much of this benefit.

My Lord, I cannot stress enough the implications of this engagement. Our current fleet, the pride of the Empire and the foundation of our global power, may well have been rendered obsolete overnight. The days of wooden warships appear to be at an end.

I strongly urge the Admiralty to immediately:

1. Commission a thorough study of both ironclad designs, with an eye towards developing our own ironclad fleet.

2. Reassess our naval strategy and tactics in light of this new technology.

3. Consider the diplomatic implications. Our ability to project power globally may be temporarily compromised until we can field our own ironclad fleet.

4. Initiate discussions with shipyards about the feasibility of rapidly constructing ironclad vessels.

Furthermore, I recommend we closely monitor the ongoing American conflict for further naval innovations. This war is rapidly becoming a testing ground for modern military technology.

I await your instructions on how to proceed.

Your obedient servant,

Captain Sir Alexander Milne

P.S. On a personal note, my Lord, I must confess that witnessing the aftermath of this battle and hearing the accounts of those present has left me profoundly unsettled. In all my years of naval service, I have never seen anything to rival the destructive power of these ironclads. The sight of the USS Cumberland's masts protruding from the waters of Hampton Roads, all that remains of a once-proud warship, is a chilling reminder of how quickly the tides of naval supremacy can turn. We must act swiftly and decisively if we are to maintain our dominion over the seas.

INTERNAL MEMORANDUM

To: First Sea Lord, Vice-Admiral Sir Richard Saunders Dundas
From: Naval Intelligence Division
Date: 20 March 1862

Sir,

Having analyzed Captain Milne's report and the accompanying documents regarding the ironclad engagement at Hampton Roads, we offer the following observations:

1. The battle confirms our own experiments with iron-hulled vessels and suggests we must accelerate our ironclad program.

2. The rotating turret of the Monitor merits particular attention. It solves many problems of broadside armament and should be studied closely.

3. Both vessels' reduced crews suggest potential for manpower efficiency in future naval engagements.

4. The psychological impact of these seemingly invulnerable ships on enemy forces cannot be overstated.

5. We must consider that other naval powers, particularly France and Russia, will also be drawing lessons from this engagement.

Recommendations:

1. Dispatch naval engineers to the United States under the guise of neutral observers to gather more detailed information on ironclad construction and performance.

2. Increase funding for our own ironclad development programs, particularly those of chief constructor Edward Reed.

3. Begin war game scenarios incorporating ironclad vessels to develop new tactics.

4. Consider how this development might affect our global strategy, particularly in more confined waters like the Mediterranean or the Baltic.

The American Civil War has ushered in a new era of naval warfare. We must adapt swiftly to maintain our naval supremacy.

Respectfully submitted,

Naval Intelligence Division

Chapter 22

The Hornet's Nest

The Battle of Shiloh, April 1862

April 6, 1862 - Dawn

The mist clings to the ground like a shroud, obscuring the feet of my men as they move into position. I, General Albert Sidney Johnston, commander of the Confederate Army of Mississippi, survey the scene before me. In the distance, through the trees and fog, lie the unsuspecting Union forces under General Grant. They have no idea what's about to hit them.

I turn to my aide. "Send word to Generals Hardee and Bragg. We attack in fifteen minutes."

As he rushes off, I allow myself a moment of grim satisfaction. We've achieved complete surprise. Grant thinks we're still in Corinth, but here we are, ready to strike like a thunderbolt from a clear sky.

The sound of a twig snapping makes me turn. It's General Beauregard, looking concerned.

"General Johnston," he says, "don't you think the element of surprise is lost? The enemy must have heard our approach."

I shake my head. "I would fight them if they were a million. We will attack them today and smash them before Grant and Buell can unite."

Beauregard doesn't look convinced, but there's no time for debate. The die is cast.

Suddenly, the relative quiet of the morning is shattered by the boom of artillery. Hardee's corps has engaged the enemy. The Battle of Shiloh has begun.

I spur my horse forward, moving with the advancing troops. The initial confusion among the Union forces is palpable. Everywhere I look, blue-clad soldiers are scrambling for their weapons, many still in their nightshirts.

"Press on, men!" I shout, my voice carrying over the growing din of battle. "Drive them into the Tennessee!"

As the morning wears on, the fighting intensifies. Reports come in of fierce resistance in a sunken road that the men are calling the "Hornet's Nest." I decide to personally lead a charge to break this strongpoint.

The air is thick with gun smoke and the screams of the wounded. A bullet whizzes past my head, but I pay it no mind. I've been in too many battles to flinch at such things now.

As I ride along the line, encouraging the men, I feel a sharp sting in my right leg. Looking down, I see a small tear in my boot, seeping blood. It's nothing, I tell myself. The wound can't be serious.

But as the minutes tick by, I begin to feel lightheaded. The blood loss is more severe than I thought. I turn to my aide, Governor Harris of Tennessee.

"Governor," I say, my voice weaker than I'd like, "I fear the wound is serious. Find me a surgeon."

As Harris rides off, I struggle to maintain my composure. The battle is going well, but there's still much to be done. I can't fall now, not when victory is within our grasp.

My vision begins to blur. I sway in the saddle, barely aware of the hands reaching up to steady me. As darkness closes in, my last thought is of the battle. Who will lead the men now?

I hope Beauregard is ready for what's to come...

April 6, 1862 - Late Afternoon

The news of Johnston's fall hits me like a physical blow. I, General P.G.T. Beauregard, find myself thrust into command of the Army of Mississippi in the midst of the most crucial battle of the war thus far.

"Status report," I bark to the aide who brought me the news. "What's our situation?"

As he rattles off positions and casualty estimates, my mind races. We've pushed the Federals back, yes, but they're not broken. The sun is getting low, and our men are exhausted.

I ride to the front lines, taking in the chaos of battle. The fighting around the Hornet's Nest has been particularly fierce. I can see why Johnston was so focused on breaking this point.

"General Beauregard!" A courier rides up, his horse lathered with sweat. "General Breckinridge reports heavy resistance near Pittsburg Landing. He requests reinforcements."

I weigh the options quickly. "Tell Breckinridge to hold his position. We'll renew the assault at dawn."

As twilight approaches, I make the difficult decision to call a halt to the day's fighting. Some of my subordinates protest, arguing we should press our advantage, but I stand firm. The men are spent, ammunition is low, and in the gathering darkness, we risk firing on our own troops.

That night, as I try to snatch a few hours of sleep, the sounds of steamboats on the Tennessee River reach my ears. Buell's reinforcements are arriving. Tomorrow will be a different battle entirely.

April 7, 1862 - Dawn

The attack that greets us at first light is ferocious. Grant and Buell's combined forces hit our lines like a sledgehammer. I quickly realize we're now on the defensive.

"Pull Breckinridge's division back to support our center," I order, watching as the blue-clad troops push our men back from the ground we'd taken yesterday.

The fighting is intense, but I can see we're losing ground. By midday, it's clear that we can't hold. The cost in lives would be too great.

With a heavy heart, I give the order to begin an orderly withdrawal back to Corinth. As we retreat, I can't help but wonder: if Johnston had lived, could we have won the day yesterday? Would it have made a difference today?

But such thoughts are useless now. We've bloodied the Federals badly, even if we couldn't deliver the knockout blow we'd hoped for. This battle has changed the war, I'm certain of it. The days of gentlemanly conflict are over. Shiloh has ushered in a new era of bloodshed that I fear will consume us all.

As we march south, the rain begins to fall, as if the very heavens are weeping for the thousands of young men left dead and dying on the fields behind us. Shiloh Church, once a place of peace, now stands as a silent witness to the carnage of these two terrible days.

The Battle of Shiloh is over, but the war, I fear, has only just begun.

Chapter 23

The Rise of Robert E. Lee

Richmond's Deliverance, May/June 1862

May 31, 1862 - Richmond, Virginia

The weight of the Confederacy rests heavily upon my shoulders as I, Jefferson Davis, President of the Confederate States of America, pace the floors of the Executive Mansion. The news from the front is grim. General Joseph E. Johnston has been wounded at Seven Pines, and his performance before that left much to be desired. McClellan's army is at our doorstep, and Richmond, the heart of our nascent nation, lies vulnerable.

I pause at the window, gazing out at the city streets. The usual bustle is tinged with an undercurrent of fear. They know, as I do, how precarious our situation has become.

A knock at the door interrupts my brooding. "Enter," I call out.

My aide steps in, his face grave. "Mr. President, General Lee is here as you requested."

I nod, steeling myself for the conversation to come. "Send him in."

Robert E. Lee enters, his bearing as dignified and composed as ever. Despite the circumstances, I feel a flutter of hope. If any man can salvage this situation, it's Lee.

"General," I greet him, "thank you for coming so promptly. I trust you're aware of our current predicament?"

Lee nods solemnly. "Yes, Mr. President. The situation is indeed serious."

I move to my desk, picking up a dispatch. "Johnston's wounding has left us without a commander at this critical juncture. I've been considering our options, and I believe the time has come for you to take command of the army."

Lee's expression remains impassive, but I detect a flicker of something in his eyes. Concern? Determination? It's hard to say.

"Mr. President," he replies carefully, "I am, of course, at the service of the Confederacy. But are you certain I'm the right man for this task? There are others with more field experience."

I shake my head firmly. "None I trust more than you, Robert. But before we make this official, I'd like to ride out to the lines with you. I need to see the situation for myself, and I value your perspective."

Lee nods his assent, and within the hour, we're on horseback, riding towards the scene of yesterday's battle. As we leave the city behind, I can't help but wonder: is this the man who will save Richmond, and with it, our cause? Only time will tell.

As we ride towards the battlefield, the signs of recent combat become increasingly evident. The air is thick with the acrid smell of gunpowder, and the distant sound of sporadic gunfire punctuates our conversation.

"Tell me, General," I begin, breaking the silence, "what are your thoughts on our current strategy?"

Lee is quiet for a moment, his eyes scanning the terrain. "Mr. President, our current defensive posture, while understandable, is ultimately untenable. McClellan outnumbers us significantly, and each day he draws his noose tighter around Richmond."

I nod, encouraging him to continue.

"We cannot simply react to the enemy's movements," Lee adds, his voice gaining conviction. "We must seize the initiative, force McClellan to defend himself rather than press his advantage."

"An offensive?" I ask, intrigued. "But how, Robert? We're outnumbered and, if reports are correct, outgunned."

Lee's eyes meet mine, and I see a fire there that I haven't noticed before. "We may be outnumbered, sir, but we are not outmaneuvered. Not yet. McClellan is cautious to a fault. We can use that against him."

As we crest a hill, the full extent of yesterday's battle becomes clear. The field before us is littered with the debris of war—discarded equipment, fallen trees, and, more somberly, the bodies of the fallen not yet recovered.

Lee continues, his voice low but intense. "I propose we bring in reinforcements from wherever we can spare them. Jackson's force in the Valley, troops from the Carolinas. Then, we hit McClellan's right flank with everything we have."

"It's risky," I muse, considering the audacity of the plan. "If it fails, Richmond could fall."

"Yes, Mr. President," Lee acknowledges. "But if we do nothing, Richmond will certainly fall. Sometimes, the boldest move is the safest."

As we turn our horses back toward Richmond, I feel a sense of clarity I haven't experienced in weeks. "Very well, Robert. I'm entrusting the defense of our capital—indeed, the fate of our nation—to you. You'll have operational control of all forces in the vicinity of Richmond."

Lee straightens in his saddle, the weight of responsibility settling visibly on his shoulders. "I'll do my utmost to prove worthy of your trust, Mr. President."

As the spires of Richmond come back into view, I can't help but feel a renewed sense of hope. In Lee, we may have found not just a general, but a savior for our beleaguered nation.

"Godspeed, General Lee," I say as we part ways at the edge of the city. "The prayers of the Confederacy go with you."

June 1, 1862 - Confederate Headquarters, Richmond

The candle flickers as I, Robert E. Lee, pore over the maps spread across my desk. The responsibility President Davis has placed upon me weighs heavily, but I feel a sense of clarity I haven't experienced in months.

To save Richmond, we must do more than defend—we must attack.

I trace the blue lines representing McClellan's forces on the map. His army is split by the Chickahominy River, a weakness we must exploit. But to do so, I need more men.

I reach for a fresh sheet of paper and begin to write:

"To General Jackson,

You are to move with all possible speed from the Valley to join us at Richmond. Maintain utmost secrecy. The enemy must not suspect your departure..."

Jackson's arrival could be the key to our success. With his forces, we might just have enough strength to drive McClellan back.

My mind races with the possibilities. We'll need to strike hard and fast, giving McClellan no time to consolidate his forces. A series of attacks, each one building on the last, keeping the Federals off-balance and reeling.

I allow myself a small smile. Little Mac, as they call him, is a skilled organizer but overly cautious. We can use that against him. If we can rattle him, make him believe he's outnumbered, he might just retreat all the way back to Washington.

But the risks are enormous. If we fail, Richmond falls. If Richmond falls, our cause may well be lost. The fate of the Confederacy could hinge on the coming days.

I lean back in my chair, feeling the weight of the moment. I think of my family's plantation at Arlington, now in enemy hands. Of my conflicted decision to resign from the U.S. Army and cast my lot with Virginia. Of the men—on both sides—who have already given their lives in this terrible conflict.

"God of our fathers," I whisper, bowing my head, "grant us victory if we are worthy. If not, then let us never lack the courage to face whatever may come."

With renewed determination, I turn back to my maps. There is much to do, and precious little time. The next week will determine the fate of Richmond, and perhaps the war itself.

I pray we are equal to the task.

****

In the weeks that followed, Lee's audacious plan unfolded in what became known as the Seven Days Battles. From June 25 to July 1, 1862, Lee's Army of Northern Virginia launched a series of attacks against McClellan's forces, driving them away from Richmond in a campaign that would become legendary.

Though not an unqualified victory, Lee's aggressive tactics succeeded in lifting the siege of Richmond and pushing McClellan's army back to the James River. This remarkable turnaround not only saved the Confederate capital but also established Robert E. Lee as a brilliant tactician and a hero of the South. The Seven Days Battles marked a turning point in the Eastern Theater of the war, shifting momentum to the Confederates and setting the stage for Lee's future campaigns that would keep the Union at bay for two more years.

Chapter 24

Letter from Frederick Douglass to Abraham Lincoln, August 1862

August 15, 1862

His Excellency Abraham Lincoln
President of the United States
Washington, D.C.

Mr. President,

I write to you today not merely as a private citizen, but as a voice for millions of enslaved souls who cannot speak for themselves. The war which now engulfs our nation has reached a critical juncture, and I implore you to seize this moment to align the Union's cause with the cause of universal human freedom.

Sir, the time has come for a bold proclamation of emancipation. I understand the delicate nature of your position and the myriad political considerations you must weigh. However, I believe that a preliminary declaration, to be followed by a legally binding proclamation, would serve both moral and strategic purposes.

Such a declaration would accomplish several crucial objectives:

1). It would transform this conflict from a war solely for the Union into a war for human liberty, thus claiming the moral high ground and potentially swaying European opinion in our favor.

2). It would strike at the very foundation of the Confederacy's strength by undermining their labor force and potentially inciting unrest within their borders.

3). It would energize the Northern populace, many of whom yearn to see this war fought for a higher purpose than mere reunification.

4). It would open the door for the enlistment of colored troops, a vast untapped resource of loyal and motivated soldiers for the Union cause.

I propose, Mr. President, that you issue a preliminary proclamation forthwith, declaring your intent to emancipate all slaves in rebellious states effective January 1, 1863. This would give the Confederate states fair warning and an opportunity to lay down their arms and return to the Union fold.

Furthermore, I urge you to consider extending this emancipation to all slaves within the United States, including those in border states. I understand the political risks inherent in such a move, but half-measures will not suffice in this great moral struggle.

Lastly, I beseech you to consider the future of these soon-to-be freed individuals. Emancipation must be accompanied by a commitment to full citizenship rights, including the right to vote, serve on juries, and enjoy equal protection under the law.

Mr. President, history has placed you in a position to not only save the Union but to purge it of its greatest sin. I pray you will rise to this monumental occasion.

I remain, sir, your obedient servant,

Frederick Douglass

Chapter 25

The Weight of Freedom

Lincoln's Emancipation Dilemma, September 1862

September 22, 1862 - The White House, Washington D.C.

I, Abraham Lincoln, sit alone in my office, Douglass's impassioned letter spread before me. The weight of the decision I'm about to make feels heavier than the entire war itself.

Emancipation. The very word carries with it the power to reshape our nation, for better or worse. But how to implement it without shattering the fragile coalition that keeps the Union together?

I pick up my pen and begin to jot down my thoughts:

1. Scope of Emancipation:

- Cannot include border states still in the Union (Kentucky, Missouri, Maryland, Delaware)

- Reasoning: Risk of pushing these states into the Confederacy

- Political reality: Need their support to maintain war effort

- Personal belief: Preserving the Union must come first; without it, emancipation is moot

I pause, considering the backlash this limitation will surely provoke from abolitionists like Douglass. But I must be pragmatic. This war cannot be won without the border states.

2. Areas under Union control:

- Cannot include areas already under Union control in Confederate states

- Reasoning: Need legal justification as a war measure

- Can only apply to areas in active rebellion

Another difficult decision, but necessary. I cannot overstep my constitutional authority as Commander-in-Chief.

3. Timing:

- Issue preliminary proclamation now, effective January 1, 1863

- Gives 100 days for Confederate states to return to Union

- Allows time to gauge public and international reaction

4. Citizenship and voting rights:

- Cannot include guarantee of full citizenship or voting rights

- Reasoning: Too controversial, could lose support of conservative Republicans and War Democrats

- Personal view: A step too far at this moment, but a goal for the future

My hand cramps as I write this last point. How I wish I could grant Douglass's full request, to sweep away the injustice of slavery in one grand gesture. But the harsh reality of politics and the fragile state of the Union demand a more measured approach.

I lean back, exhausted. This proclamation will be denounced as too radical by some, too limited by others. But it is, I believe, the furthest I can go at this moment in history.

As Commander-in-Chief, I have the authority to seize enemy property as a war measure. By defining slaves in rebellious states as such, I can legally justify their emancipation. It's not perfect, but it's a start.

I begin to draft the proclamation, choosing my words carefully. This document will change the character of the war, transforming it from a fight merely to preserve the Union to a struggle for human freedom.

Yet even as I write, I'm acutely aware of the proclamation's limitations. It will not free a single slave in the border states or in areas under Union control. It offers no guarantee of citizenship or voting rights. It is, in many ways, more symbolic than immediately effective.

But symbols have power. This proclamation will be a promise—to the slaves, to the nation, and to posterity—that from this day forward, the United States moves inexorably toward universal freedom.

As I sign the preliminary proclamation, I whisper a silent prayer. May God grant that this be the first step toward justice for all, and may He give us the strength to see it through to its full realization.

Chapter 26

A Desperate Gambit

Davis Responds to Lincoln's Proclamation, September 1862

Richmond, Virginia - September 24, 1862

I, Jefferson Davis, President of the Confederate States of America, crumple the telegram in my fist, a mirthless laugh escaping my lips. Lincoln's latest ploy—this so-called "Preliminary Emancipation Proclamation"—is as desperate as it is insulting.

"Does he truly believe this will sway us?" I mutter, pacing my office. The proclamation, issued just two days ago, promises to free slaves in Confederate states if we do not return to the Union by January 1, 1863. It's a transparent attempt to fracture our resolve, to lure states back with the promise of maintaining slavery.

I call for my secretary. "Prepare a statement for immediate release," I instruct him. "Make it clear that the Confederate States categorically reject this underhanded attempt at coercion."

As he scribbles, I dictate: "Mr. Lincoln's proclamation is a mere paper declaration, without legal force, aimed at inciting servile insurrection. It serves only to confirm the true nature of the war the United States wages against us—a war of subjugation and destruction of our way of life."

I pause, considering the broader implications. "Add this: The Confederacy reaffirms its commitment to independence. We will not be lured back into a Union that threatens the very foundations of our society and economy."

As my secretary departs to distribute the statement, I turn to the window, gazing out at Richmond. Lincoln's gambit changes nothing. If anything, it will only steel the resolve of our people, uniting them against this latest Yankee aggression.

I pause, considering the international implications of Lincoln's proclamation. "This may complicate our efforts to gain recognition from Britain and France," I muse. "They may find it harder to support our cause if Lincoln successfully paints this war as a crusade against slavery. We must reinforce our message that this is a war for independence, not for the preservation of any particular institution."

My mind turns to the potential impact within our own borders. While I'm confident in the loyalty of our slave population, we must be vigilant. "We should instruct governors to increase patrols and tighten security," I note to myself. "Not out of fear, but as a precaution against any misguided souls who might take Lincoln's words as a call to action."

Let Lincoln free the slaves he cannot reach. We will fight on, more determined than ever to secure our independence and preserve our way of life.

Chapter 27

The Earth Cries Out

Antietam's Bloody Harvest, September 1862

I am the soil of Antietam, and I remember.

For countless seasons, I nurtured life. My fertile expanse stretched across gentle hills and shallow valleys, embracing the meandering Antietam Creek. Generations of farmers tilled my flesh, and I gave them bountiful harvests. Corn stalks swayed in summer breezes, their roots tickling my depths. Wheat fields rippled like golden oceans under azure skies. Children's laughter echoed as they played among the apple orchards and sunflower patches.

Peace was my constant companion, broken only by the rhythmic fall of plowshares and the patter of gentle rains.

But now, on this September morning in 1862, I tremble with foreboding. For days, I have felt the approach of something monstrous. The distant rumble of thousands upon thousands of feet grows ever closer. The weight of iron and wood—gun carriages and caissons—presses into me, tearing up the crops I've so lovingly nurtured.

Men in blue and gray swarm across my surface like ants, their nervous energy seeping into my very core. They dig and scratch at me, carving trenches and rifle pits. Their fear is palpable, an acrid taste that mingles with the morning dew.

In the pre-dawn stillness, I feel them shift and stir. Tens of thousands of hearts beat in anticipation, their rhythms thrumming through my being. The air is thick with tension, like the moments before a thunderstorm breaks.

Then, suddenly, hell is unleashed upon my peaceful fields.

The first cannon's roar shakes me to my bedrock. A thousand more join the chorus, their shells tearing through flesh and soil alike. Feet pound across me in great waves as men charge forward, then fall back, then charge again.

I feel every footfall, every stumble, every body that crashes to the ground. Blue and gray, North and South—to me, they are all the same. All are my children, and all are dying.

Their hot blood seeps into me, carrying with it final thoughts of home, of mothers, of sweethearts left behind. I try to comfort them in their last moments, to cradle them as they sink into my embrace. But there are so many. So very many.

In the Miller's cornfield, men fall like wheat before the scythe. By the Dunker Church, waves of humanity crash against each other, breaking and reforming like a tide of death. Along Bloody Lane, bodies pile atop one another until the dirt can no longer be seen beneath the dead and dying.

And still, they come. Still, they fall. Still, I drink their blood and receive their bodies, blue and gray alike.

I am the soil of Antietam, and today, I weep.

As the sun climbs higher, its warmth a cruel contrast to the coldness of death spreading across my surface, the fury of the battle reaches its zenith. I shudder beneath the weight of so much suffering, so much loss.

At the center of my being, where a simple sunken road once offered respite to weary travelers, a maelstrom of destruction now rages. Men call it Bloody Lane, and oh, how it lives up to that grim name. Bodies fall in heaps, slipping and sliding in the gore-slicked earth. I try to hold onto them all, to give them one last moment of stability in the chaos, but there are too many. They pile atop one another, dead eyes staring sightlessly at the uncaring sky.

Near the creek that bears my name, a stone bridge becomes the focal point of unimaginable courage and unspeakable carnage. Men in blue charge again and again, their bodies falling into the cool waters that once nourished my fields. The creek runs red, carrying the lifeblood of a divided nation downstream.

Throughout this longest of days, I feel every impact, every loss. A young boy, barely old enough to hold a rifle, whispers his mother's name as he breathes his last into my soil. A grizzled veteran, survivor of a dozen battles, finally meets his end and sinks into my embrace. Limbs torn from bodies, lives cut brutally short—I cradle them all, blue and gray alike.

As evening approaches, the fury begins to ebb. The constant thunder of guns fades to sporadic fire, then to an eerie silence broken only by the moans of the wounded and dying. I feel the survivors moving slowly across my torn and bloodied surface, searching for fallen comrades, for scraps of hope in a landscape of despair.

Night falls, and still I bleed. The blood of 22,717 Americans—brothers, fathers, sons—seeps deep into my core. It carries with it dreams unfulfilled, promises unkept, futures forever lost.

In a single day, I have become a vast cemetery, a testament to the high cost of a nation divided against itself.

Even as the battle ends, I know that my transformation is permanent. Never again will I be simply peaceful farmland. I am now hallowed ground, sanctified by sacrifice, forever changed by this single day of unimaginable bloodshed.

The dead will be buried, the armies will move on, but I will remember. Every season, every year, every generation—I will hold these memories. When the corn grows again, it will be nourished by the blood spilled this day. When children play in these fields in years to come, they will run unknowing above the remains of heroes.

I am the soil of Antietam. I am a battlefield, a graveyard, a memorial. And I will bear witness, for all time, to both the depths of human cruelty and the heights of human courage. May my blood-soaked fields one day yield a harvest of peace.

Chapter 28

A Year of Change

Elias and Jeremiah Face New Realities, December 1862

Boston, Massachusetts - December 28, 1862

Elias Merriweather stood behind the counter of his general store, absently polishing the same spot on the worn wood. The shop was quiet, a far cry from the bustling business of peacetime. War had changed everything.

"Pa?" Emily's voice broke through his reverie. "Another letter from Thomas."

Elias took the envelope with trembling hands. Since Thomas had joined the army after Antietam, every letter was a relief and a source of fresh worry.

"He's safe," Elias announced after scanning the contents. "Still in training camp."

Sarah emerged from the back room, flour dusting her apron. "Thank the Lord," she murmured.

As Emily returned to helping her mother, Elias's mind wandered to the events of the past year. The bloodbath at Antietam had shocked the nation, pushing Lincoln to issue his Emancipation Proclamation. Elias remembered the heated debates in the shop when news of the preliminary proclamation arrived.

"It's about time," old Mr. Johnson had declared. "Make this war mean something."

But others weren't so sure. "What about the economy?" young Peters had argued. "Who'll pick the cotton?"

Elias sighed, looking at the sparse shelves. The war had been good for some businesses, but a general store felt every shortage. Coffee was scarce, sugar prices had skyrocketed, and textile goods were becoming harder to source.

Still, as he watched Sarah and Emily work, Elias felt a surge of pride. They'd adapted, learned to make do with less. And Thomas...well, Thomas was fighting for a cause greater than himself.

"1863 has to be better," Elias murmured. "It just has to be."

****

Outside Atlanta, Georgia - December 30, 1862

Jeremiah Calhoun squinted at the fading light, willing the sun to stay up just a bit longer. Every moment of daylight was precious now, with so much work and so few hands to do it.

"Pa!" James called from the barn. "Buttercup's not looking good. Think it's the colic again."

Jeremiah cursed under his breath. They couldn't afford to lose another cow. Not with prices what they were and supplies so hard to come by.

As he strode toward the barn, the weight of the past year pressed down on him. The damn Yankees and their blockade had choked off trade, leaving store shelves bare and fields untended as more and more men marched off to war.

William's last letter sat heavily in Jeremiah's pocket. His eldest had fought at Antietam, surviving that bloodbath by the grace of God. But the boy's words spoke of weariness, of horrors Jeremiah could scarcely imagine.

And now this "Emancipation Proclamation" of Lincoln's. The news had spread like wildfire, causing unrest among the slaves in neighboring plantations. Jeremiah's small farm didn't rely on slave labor, but he feared the broader implications.

"It'll tear the whole economy apart," he'd argued at the last town meeting. "And for what? To incite slave rebellions while we're too busy fighting to defend ourselves?"

Inside the barn, James looked up from Buttercup's stall, his young face etched with worry. "What're we gonna do, Pa?"

Jeremiah placed a calloused hand on his son's shoulder. "We'll do what we've always done, son. Endure."

As they tended to the ailing cow, Jeremiah's mind turned to the coming year. Surely, 1863 would bring victory for the Confederacy. It had to. The alternative was too painful to consider.

****

As the sun set on 1862, both Elias Merriweather and Jeremiah Calhoun stood on the cusp of a new year, each man hoping for victory, for peace, for the safe return of their sons. Neither could know the trials that 1863 would bring, nor the profound changes that would reshape their nation forever.

1863

Chapter 29

Freedom's Dawn: Echoes of Emancipation

The Emancipation Proclamation, January 1, 1863

Union Camp near the Virginia border - Dawn, January 1, 1863

Sergeant John Miller's hands shook as he unfolded the rain-speckled newspaper, the weight of history heavy in his calloused hands. The pale winter sun was just beginning to peek over the horizon, casting long shadows across the muddy camp.

"Listen up, boys," he called, his voice cracking with emotion. As he read Lincoln's words aloud, the camp came alive with a cacophony of reactions. Cheers and curses mingled in the crisp morning air.

Corporal Thompson's eyes shone with unshed tears. "About time," he growled, his voice thick. "Now we're fighting for something real. Something my pa would've been proud of."

But Private Jenkins spat on the frozen ground, his face twisted in disgust. "I didn't sign up to free no slaves. My family's struggling back home, and we're here risking our necks for this?"

The sergeant's voice cut through the growing argument, steady but tinged with awe. "It says here all slaves in rebellious states are free. Doesn't matter what we signed up for. These are our orders now." He paused, looking each man in the eye. "Boys, we're part of history now. For better or worse."

Charleston, South Carolina - Midday

The grandfather clock in Edward Rutledge's study chimed noon as he crumpled the telegram in his fist, his knuckles white with rage. "Damn that Lincoln," he snarled, turning to his house slave, Samuel, who stood frozen by the door. "He thinks he can incite insurrection? We'll see about that."

Samuel's heart raced, but he kept his face impassive. Freedom? Could it be true? As he quietly backed out of the room, Rutledge reached for his coat, muttering, "I must warn the others. This changes everything."

Once in the hallway, Samuel leaned against the wall, his mind reeling. He had to tell the others, but caution was key. One wrong move now could be fatal.

Confederate Camp outside Richmond - Afternoon

Lieutenant Thomas Garland lowered the dispatch, his face a mask of disbelief. "Lincoln's freed the slaves? In states he doesn't even control?"

Private Willoughby sneered, "It's a bluff, sir. Trying to stir up trouble behind our lines."

Garland wasn't so sure. "Maybe. But if those slaves believe it..." He left the thought unfinished, a chill running down his spine despite the afternoon heat.

London, England - Evening

In his study, American ambassador Charles Francis Adams penned a hurried note to Secretary of State William Seward, the scratching of his quill punctuating the ticking of the mantel clock.

"Initial reactions mixed," he wrote, brow furrowed. "Some hail it as a moral triumph, others decry it as an act of desperation. Its impact on British intervention remains uncertain." He paused, then added, "The tide of opinion here may be turning in our favor, but we must tread carefully."

Boston, Massachusetts - Night

William Lloyd Garrison's hands trembled as he read the Proclamation by lamplight, the paper crinkling under his tight grip. Tears sprang to the old abolitionist's eyes, and a lifetime of struggle seemed to pass before him.

"It's not perfect," he murmured, his voice choked with emotion. "But it's a start. After all these years, it's finally a start." He looked up at the portrait of Frederick Douglass on his wall. "We did it, old friend. We've lived to see this day."

Slave Quarters, Plantation outside Richmond, Virginia - Midnight

In the cramped, musty slave quarters, a dozen faces gleamed in the faint light of a single candle. The air was thick with anticipation and fear. Old Sam, his weathered face etched with years of hardship, leancd forward.

"Heard it from Massa's house," he whispered, his voice trembling. "Lincoln done said we's free."

A ripple of gasps and murmurs swept through the room. Young Bessie clutched her baby closer, her eyes wide. "Free? What that mean for us, Sam?"

"Means we ain't property no more," Sam replied, his voice thick with emotion. "Leastways, that's what it's supposed to mean."

"But how?" asked Tom, a field hand with calloused hands, his tone skeptical. "Massa ain't just gonna let us walk away."

Sarah, known for her caution, shook her head, fear evident in her voice. "And where would we go? Yankees ain't here. Who's gonna enforce this?"

"Maybe we should run," suggested Jacob, the youngest of the group, excitement and terror warring in his eyes. "Head north, find the Union army."

A tense silence fell. The enormity of what lay before them—the hope, the danger, the unknown—weighed heavily in the air. The creaking of the old cabin and the muffled sobs of those overcome with emotion were the only sounds.

Finally, Mary, the oldest among them, spoke up, her voice quavering but resolute. "We's been prayin' for this day. Maybe it ain't perfect. Maybe it ain't safe. But it's a chance, children. A chance our folks ain't never had before."

Sam nodded solemnly, tears glistening in his eyes. "We gotta be careful. Smart. But Mary's right. This here's our chance. Freedom's comin', sure as dawn."

As the group dispersed, slipping silently back to their quarters, the word "freedom" echoed in whispers, a dangerous hope taking root in the heart of the night. Each step was cautious, each breath measured, as they carried the weight of generations' dreams on their shoulders.

In the distance, a rooster crowed, heralding the arrival of a new day—and perhaps, a new era.

Chapter 30

The Fall of a Giant

Stonewall's Last March, May 1863

Richmond, Virginia - May 15, 1863

A heavy silence blanketed the streets of Richmond as the funeral procession wound its way through the Confederate capital. The rhythmic clop of horses' hooves and the muffled drumbeat seemed to echo the heartbeat of a nation in mourning. Thousands lined the route, heads bowed, as the flag-draped coffin of Lieutenant General Thomas J. "Stonewall" Jackson passed by.

At the graveside, General Robert E. Lee stood rigid, his face a mask of grief and composure. As the crowd settled, he stepped forward, his voice carrying across the hushed gathering.

"We are gathered here today to bid farewell not just to a soldier, but to a legend. Thomas Jonathan Jackson was more than a general; he was the very embodiment of our cause, a living testament to the strength and resolve of the Confederate States of America."

Lee paused, his gaze sweeping over the assembled mourners—soldiers, politicians, and civilians alike, united in their loss.

"It was but two weeks ago that General Jackson demonstrated once again the brilliance that earned him the name 'Stonewall.' At Chancellorsville, we faced an enemy that outnumbered us two to one. General Hooker's army of 130,000 men threatened to overwhelm our position. Victory seemed all but impossible."

Lee's voice grew stronger as he recounted the battle, painting a vivid picture of that fateful day.

"But Stonewall Jackson saw an opportunity where others saw only peril. He came to me with a bold plan—to march his entire corps around the enemy's flank, to strike where they least expected. It was a maneuver fraught with risk, leaving our lines dangerously thin. Yet, such was my trust in Jackson that I approved his audacious scheme."

The crowd hung on Lee's every word, reliving the recent triumph and tragedy through their commander's eyes.

"On May 2nd, as the sun began to set, Jackson's men crashed into the Union right flank like a thunderbolt. The enemy, caught unawares, broke and ran. It was a moment of supreme victory, a testament to the tactical genius of the man we honor today."

Lee's voice faltered slightly as he continued, "And yet, in the very hour of his greatest triumph, fate struck a cruel blow. As night fell and the fighting died down, General Jackson rode out to reconnoiter the enemy's position, planning for the next day's assault that would complete our victory."

The general's eyes closed briefly, reliving the moment. "In the darkness and confusion, a group of our own men, mistaking Jackson and his staff for enemy cavalry, opened fire. Our great Stonewall fell, struck by three bullets."

A collective gasp rose from the crowd, many hearing the detailed account for the first time.

"Even then, in his final conscious moments, Jackson's thoughts were of duty and victory. 'Order A.P. Hill to prepare for action,' he commanded. 'We must hold our ground.' Such was the indomitable spirit of the man."

Lee paused, allowing the weight of the moment to settle over the assembly.

"For a week, we dared to hope. The battle was won—Hooker's great army was forced to retreat across the Rappahannock, leaving behind 17,000 casualties to our 13,000. It was a victory that shall echo through history, a testament to Confederate arms and to Jackson's tactical genius."

"But even as we celebrated, our joy was tempered by concern for our fallen leader. Pneumonia set in, and on May 10th, Stonewall Jackson offered up his soul to his Maker, his last words a fitting epitaph for a soldier of his caliber: 'Let us cross over the river, and rest under the shade of the trees.'"

Lee's gaze swept over the crowd once more, his voice gaining strength. "The loss of General Jackson is a grievous blow, not just to our army, but to our entire cause. He was the right arm of this army, a commander whose very name struck fear into the heart of our enemies."

"Yet, we must not falter. The cause for which Stonewall Jackson gave his life still hangs in the balance. The victory at Chancellorsville, bought with his blood and the blood of thousands of brave Confederate soldiers, has opened new possibilities for our struggle."

Lee straightened, his voice ringing out with resolve. "In the coming days, we will carry the fight to the enemy. We will march north, into Pennsylvania, forcing the Federals to meet us on ground of our choosing. And when we do, the spirit of Stonewall Jackson will march with us."

"Let us honor his memory not with tears alone, but with a renewed commitment to the cause of Southern independence. In life, General Jackson was our strength. In death, let him be our inspiration."

As Lee stepped back, a bugler sounded "Taps," its mournful notes drifting over the silent crowd. The first handful of earth fell upon Jackson's coffin, and with it, the last embers of the Confederacy's invincibility were laid to rest.

****

The Battle of Chancellorsville had been won, but at a cost that would echo through the remaining years of the war. As the crowd slowly dispersed, the shadow of the coming campaign in the North loomed large, a campaign that would test the Confederacy as never before—a campaign without Stonewall.

Chapter 31

A Chance to Fight

The Call for Black Soldiers, May 1863

Philadelphia, Pennsylvania - May 1863

The basement of Bethel AME Church hummed with tension. Men packed the room, their faces a mix of hope, skepticism, and barely contained anger. Some wore the threadbare clothes of laborers, others the neat attire of businessmen, but all shared the weight of generations of oppression.

Isaiah Thompson, a burly dockworker with calloused hands, spoke first. "They say Lincoln's calling for us to fight. After all these years treating us like we ain't even people, now they want our blood?"

"It's a trap," muttered James Wilkins, an educated man known for his caution. "They'll put us on the front lines, use us as cannon fodder."

But Samuel Freeman, a young man with fire in his eyes, leapt to his feet. "Don't you see? This is our chance! To prove we're men, to fight for our own freedom!"

The room erupted in argument, a cacophony of voices rising and falling like waves.

Suddenly, the door burst open. A hush fell as Frederick Douglass strode in, his presence commanding instant respect. He surveyed the room, his eyes taking in the hope and fear written on every face.

"Gentlemen," Douglass began, his deep voice resonating in the small space, "I've just come from Washington. I've spoken with President Lincoln himself. The time has come for us to take up arms, not just for the Union, but for ourselves."

He paused, letting his words sink in. "For years, they told us we weren't men enough to fight. Now, we have the chance to prove them wrong. To show that we're not just fit to be slaves, but to be citizens, to be soldiers, to be free."

Isaiah spoke up, his voice rough with emotion. "But Mr. Douglass, why should we die for a country that's never cared about us?"

Douglass nodded, acknowledging the pain behind the question. "We fight not just for the country as it is, but for what it could be. Every Black man in uniform chips away at the foundations of slavery. Every drop of Black blood spilled in battle washes away the stain of centuries of bondage."

He looked around the room, meeting each man's gaze. "I won't lie to you. It will be hard. You'll face prejudice from your fellow soldiers, danger from the enemy. But remember this: once let the black man get upon his person the brass letters U.S., let him get an eagle on his button, and a musket on his shoulder and bullets in his pocket, and there is no power on earth which can deny that he has earned the right to citizenship."

As Douglass's words faded, a new energy filled the room. Men began to nod, to straighten their backs. Samuel Freeman stepped forward, chin held high.

"Where do I sign up?"

As Samuel's declaration hung in the air, other men began to step forward. Isaiah Thompson, the skeptical dockworker, stood slowly. "I still ain't sure about this," he said, his voice gruff. "But if we don't fight for ourselves, who will?"

James Wilkins, the cautious educated man, remained seated, shaking his head. "You're all rushing to your doom," he muttered, but his words were lost in the growing excitement.

The recruitment office was a converted storefront on Lombard Street. A line of black men stretched around the block, each waiting for their chance to sign up. Samuel Freeman stood near the front, practically vibrating with anticipation.

Inside, a harried-looking white sergeant sat behind a desk. "Name?" he barked as Samuel stepped forward.

"Samuel Freeman, sir."

The sergeant gave him a once-over. "Age?"

"Twenty-two, sir."

After a series of questions and a cursory physical examination, the sergeant nodded. "You'll do. Report to Camp William Penn in two days."

As Samuel left, clutching his enlistment papers, he passed Isaiah in line. They exchanged nods, a mix of excitement and apprehension in their eyes.

Not everyone was as fortunate. Further back, a man was arguing with another recruiter. "What do you mean, I'm too old? I'm strong as an ox!"

"Rules are rules," the recruiter replied, not unkindly. "We need young men who can endure the rigors of training and battle."

Camp William Penn was a shock to the system. The new recruits, used to city life, found themselves in a world of mud, mosquitoes, and endless drills.

"Left, left, left right left!" The drill sergeant's voice carried across the parade ground. Samuel and Isaiah, along with dozens of other men, marched in ragged formation.

"You call that marching?" the sergeant bellowed. "My grandmother could do better, and she's been dead for ten years!"

Despite the harsh treatment, a sense of purpose filled the air. These men were soldiers now, preparing to fight for their freedom and their country.

In the mess hall, Samuel sat with Isaiah and other recruits from Philadelphia. "Did you see the rifles they gave us?" one man grumbled. "Looks like they were used in the War of 1812."

"At least you got a rifle," another replied. "Half of us are still training with wooden sticks."

Isaiah spooned up a mouthful of beans. "Food ain't much better than what we got at home. But at least here, we're earning our keep as soldiers."

One evening, as the recruits relaxed in their barracks, a courier arrived with mail. "Thompson, Isaiah Thompson!"

Isaiah took the letter with trembling hands. As he read, his face softened. "It's from my wife," he said quietly. "Says she's proud of me. Scared, but proud."

Samuel watched as other men received their letters. Some smiled, some wept quietly. All seemed to stand a little straighter afterward, reminded of why they had chosen this path.

The night before they were to ship out, the mood in the camp was solemn. Men wrote letters, cleaned their rifles, or simply sat in contemplation.

Samuel found Isaiah sitting alone, staring at a small photograph. "That your family?" he asked softly.

Isaiah nodded. "My wife and little girl. I keep thinking...what if I never see them again?"

Samuel placed a hand on his shoulder. "We're fighting so they can have a better life. So all our people can have a better life."

"You really believe that?"

"I have to," Samuel replied. "Otherwise, what are we doing here?"

The next morning, the newly formed 3rd United States Colored Infantry Regiment marched out of Camp William Penn. As they passed through Philadelphia, crowds lined the streets.

Many cheered, waving flags and shouting encouragement. "Give 'em hell, boys!" "Show those Rebs what you're made of!"

But there were jeers too. Some white faces twisted with disgust or anger at the sight of black men in uniform. "Go back to Africa!" one man shouted.

Samuel marched on, his eyes fixed ahead. He could feel the weight of history on his shoulders, the hopes and fears of generations marching with him.

As they neared the train station, Samuel caught sight of a familiar face in the crowd. It was James Wilkins, the man who had warned against enlisting. But now, Wilkins stood tall, his hat held over his heart in a gesture of respect.

The 3rd USCT boarded the trains that would take them south, toward an uncertain future. They were no longer just men, but soldiers of the Union. Whatever trials lay ahead, they would face them together, fighting not just for victory, but for the promise of freedom and equality that had eluded their people for so long.

As the train pulled out of the station, Samuel looked back at the receding city. He didn't know if he would ever see Philadelphia again, but he knew that win or lose, live or die, he and his comrades were about to change the course of history.

Chapter 32

The Mississippi Crucible

The Vicksburg Diaries of Grant and Pemberton, May – July 1863

From the personal diary of General Ulysses S. Grant:

May 18, 1863

The weight of impending battle settles on my shoulders as I watch the sun set over the Mississippi. Vicksburg's silhouette looms in the distance, a dark promise of the struggle to come. The failures of last year's campaign gnaw at me, but I push them aside. We must succeed this time. The very fate of the Union may hinge on it.

Young Sherman visited my tent earlier, his nervous energy a stark contrast to the eerie calm before the storm. We spoke of home, of Julia and the children. God, how I miss them. For a moment, I allowed myself to imagine a world without this war, but such thoughts are luxuries I cannot afford.

Tomorrow, we move on Vicksburg. If we can split the Confederacy in two, we might just see an end to this bitter conflict. The lives of thousands rest in my hands. May God grant me the wisdom to use them well.

From the journal of General John C. Pemberton:

May 20, 1863

The thunder of Union guns shatters the morning calm, a grim herald of the siege to come. As I walk the fortifications, the acrid smell of gunpowder already heavy in the air, I see determination mingled with fear in the eyes of our defenders. They know what's at stake. Vicksburg is the key to the Mississippi, and by God, we'll defend it to our last breath.

A letter arrived from Catherine this morning, her words a balm to my troubled soul. She asks about evacuation plans for the women and children. The pain of not being able to give her a reassuring answer is almost physical. We cannot evacuate—to do so would be to admit defeat before we've begun. Vicksburg must hold, whatever the cost. I pray she'll understand, and that history will justify the suffering to come.

Grant's diary:

June 7, 1863

Nineteen days into the siege, and Vicksburg has become a hell of our making. Today, I rode out to inspect our lines, the constant thud of artillery a grim backbeat to the sounds of men laboring in the trenches. Our soldiers have become moles, burrowing ever closer to the Confederate fortifications. The ingenuity of desperation is a terrible thing to behold.

The stench is overwhelming—rotting bodies, human waste, the sickly-sweet odor of gangrene. Disease spreads through our camps like wildfire, claiming more men than Confederate bullets. Each night, I hear the moans of the dying, a haunting lullaby that follows me into fitful dreams.

Yet we must press on. Vicksburg is the key to all—with it, we split the Confederacy in two. Without it, this war could drag on for years. The cost is terrible, but the alternative is unthinkable.

Tonight, as I write by candlelight, the distant boom of cannon fire reminds me of the awful responsibility I bear. How many more must die before this city falls? The weight of command is a burden that grows heavier with each passing day.

Pemberton's journal:

June 18, 1863

Vicksburg is a city of the damned. The constant shelling has driven most civilians underground, into caves dug into the hillsides. The cries of hungry children echo through streets empty of all but the dead and dying.

Food shortages have become desperate. Today, rat meat was served at my table—a delicacy now. I ate without complaint, knowing I must set an example. But in the privacy of this journal, I confess to a growing despair. Where is Johnston with his promised relief?

The men whisper of surrender, their hollow eyes and gaunt faces a silent reproach. I find it increasingly difficult to bolster their spirits when my own wavers. Yet we must hold on. Every day we resist is another day we deny Grant his victory, another day we keep the Confederacy whole.

But at what cost? The faces of the suffering haunt my dreams. May God forgive me for what I must ask of these brave men and innocent civilians.

Grant's diary:

July 3, 1863

A white flag appeared on the Confederate ramparts this morning. Pemberton has requested a parley. As I rode out to meet him, the eerie silence of a battlefield without battle pressed in around me. The no-man's land between our lines was a grotesque tableau of war's horrors—bloated corpses, shattered equipment, the earth itself blasted and scarred.

Pemberton's face was a mask of exhaustion and defeat. We spoke under an oak tree, the contrast between its natural beauty and the man-made hell surrounding us not lost on me. His request for terms was expected, but the relief I felt was tempered by a profound sadness. These men, our countrymen, fought with valor and determination. Their suffering has been immense.

Tomorrow, on our nation's birthday, Vicksburg will fall. But I find no joy in the thought, only a grim satisfaction that this phase of the war is ending. There has been enough suffering.

Pemberton's journal:

July 4, 1863

With a heavy heart, I gave the order to stack arms this morning. As I watched my brave men lay down their weapons, many openly weeping, I felt something break inside me. We fought, we suffered, we endured—and in the end, it wasn't enough.

Grant has been magnanimous in victory, allowing my men to keep their side arms and parole. His soldiers share their rations with our starving men and civilians. This kindness, somehow, makes the defeat all the more bitter.

Tonight, as the Union celebrates both independence and victory, I sit alone in my quarters for the last time. The sounds of their rejoicing carry on the wind, a stark counterpoint to the weeping I hear from the city below.

History, I fear, will judge me harshly. But faced with the prospect of further pointless suffering, I chose surrender. May God and the South forgive me. I did what I thought was right.

****

The fall of Vicksburg, coinciding with Lee's defeat at Gettysburg, marked a turning point in the war. The Confederacy, split in two, would never recover. But for the men who fought and suffered through those 47 terrible days, both victor and vanquished, the cost of this crucial victory would be etched in their memories forever.

Chapter 33

General George G. Meade

West Point Yearbook Page

THE HOWITZER - United States Military Academy, West Point
Class of 1835

GEORGE GORDON MEADE
  "The Old Snapping Turtle"
  Hometown: Philadelphia, Pennsylvania

Class Rank: 19th out of 56
Academic Achievements:
- Excellence in Mathematics and Engineering

- Commendation in Artillery Tactics

- Proficiency in French language studies

Extracurricular Activities:
- Member, Dialectic Society

- Assistant Librarian, 1834-1835

- Participant, Annual Topographical Expedition

Quote: "Duty, Honor, Country—these are not mere words, but a way of life."

Most Likely To: "Construct an impenetrable fortress in the middle of nowhere"

Comments from Peers and Instructors:
- "Meade? Sharp as a tack, but pricklier than a porcupine." - Anonymous Classmate

- "His attention to detail in engineering problems is unmatched." - Prof. Dennis H. Mahan

- "A man of few words, but when he speaks, it's worth listening." - Cadet William T. Sherman

Future Plans: Assigned to the 3rd U.S. Artillery as a Second Lieutenant. Aspirations to join the Corps of Topographical Engineers.

Notable Traits:
- Meticulous planner

- Quick temper (working on it!)

- Dry sense of humor

- Prefers actions to words

Parting Words: "May we meet again on fields of glory, defending the honor of our great nation."

Chapter 34

Voices from the Wheatfield

Gettysburg Through Three Pairs of Eyes, July 1863

On June 28, 1863, Major General George Gordon Meade awoke to unexpected news: he had been appointed commander of the Army of the Potomac. As he hastily packed his belongings, the words from his old Howitzer yearbook flashed through his mind: "Most likely to construct an impenetrable fortress in the middle of nowhere." Little did he know that in just three days, he would be tasked with doing just that on the rolling hills of a small Pennsylvania town called Gettysburg.

****

July 1, 1863 - Morning

Corporal Thomas Jenkins of the 24th Michigan Infantry wiped the sweat from his brow as he marched north along the Emmitsburg Road. The summer heat was stifling, and rumors of Confederate forces nearby had everyone on edge. "Keep it together, boys," he muttered to his squad. "The new general's counting on us."

Private William Barksdale of the 13th Mississippi Infantry crouched behind a fence, watching the dust clouds approach from the south. The Yankees were coming, just as General Lee had predicted. William's heart raced with a mixture of excitement and fear. This was it—the moment they'd bring the war to Northern soil.

General Meade hunched over his maps in the candlelit tent, his mind racing. Reports of enemy contact near Gettysburg were trickling in. "It's happening faster than we anticipated," he told his staff. "Send word to Reynolds—hold the high ground at all costs." As he issued the order, Meade felt the weight of his new command. The meticulous planning he'd honed at West Point was being put to the ultimate test.

Thomas's regiment crested a small hill, and suddenly, the air was filled with the crack of musket fire. "Contact front!" someone yelled. Thomas dropped to the ground, fumbling to load his rifle. This wasn't supposed to happen—they were just supposed to be scouting. As bullets whizzed overhead, he thought grimly, "So much for General Meade's plan."

The Yankee line wavered under the first volley. William allowed himself a small grin as he reloaded. "Pour it into 'em, boys!" his sergeant bellowed. But as William stood to fire again, he saw more Union troops appearing on the horizon. This was going to be a long day.

As the morning wore on, both Thomas and William found themselves locked in a desperate struggle, unaware that their small skirmish was about to explode into one of the largest and most consequential battles in American history...

July 1, 1863 - Afternoon

Thomas's ears rang from the constant gunfire. His unit had been pushed back to Seminary Ridge, and the situation was deteriorating rapidly. "Where's our reinforcements?" he shouted to no one in particular. The answer came in the form of a thunderous roar as Union artillery opened up behind them.

William ducked as Union shells exploded nearby. The initial Confederate success was met with fierce resistance. He watched in awe as General Heth rallied the troops. "Forward, men! Push them back!" William's legs ached as he charged forward, the taste of gunpowder bitter in his mouth.

General Meade received the news of Major General Reynolds' death with a grim expression. "Send Hancock to take command," he ordered, his mind racing through contingencies. The high ground south of Gettysburg—that would be the key. As he issued orders to concentrate the army there, Meade reflected on his old engineering professor's words: "Position is everything in warfare."

By late afternoon, Thomas found himself retreating through the streets of Gettysburg. The chaos was complete—soldiers from different units mixed together, civilians fleeing, the wounded crying out for help. As he helped a limping comrade, Thomas caught sight of a tall hill south of town. "Fall back to Cemetery Hill!" an officer was shouting. "That's where we make our stand!"

The Union troops were on the run, and William felt a surge of elation. They'd done it—driven the Yankees back! But as they reached the edge of town, his unit's advance slowed. The Union soldiers were reforming on the hills to the south, and the Confederate attacks were losing momentum. William's sergeant spat in frustration. "Damn! We almost had 'em!"

July 1, 1863 - Evening

Meade arrived on the battlefield as night fell, the sound of sporadic gunfire still echoing across the hills. He immediately set to work, positioning corps and planning defenses. "Gentlemen," he told his gathered commanders, "we will fight it out here." As he surveyed the fishhook-shaped line forming along Cemetery Ridge, Culp's Hill, and Little Round Top, Meade allowed himself a moment of grim satisfaction. His West Point training in topography was paying off.

Thomas collapsed behind a hastily constructed barricade on Cemetery Hill, utterly exhausted. The day had been a blur of retreat and desperate fighting. But now, as more Union troops poured in through the night, he felt a glimmer of hope. "The Old Snapping Turtle's got a plan," he overheard an officer say. "We'll be ready for them tomorrow."

William helped set up camp at the base of the hills now occupied by the Union army. The men around him were confident, boasting of the day's success. But as he looked up at the formidable heights, doubt gnawed at him. They'd won the day, sure, but at what cost? And what would tomorrow bring?

July 2, 1863 - Dawn

As the sun rose over Gettysburg, both Thomas and William cleaned their weapons, checked their ammunition, and prepared for the battle to come. Neither could know that they were about to participate in one of the most crucial days in American history, a day that would see heroic charges, desperate defenses, and sacrifice beyond measure...

July 2, 1863 - Midday

Thomas wiped sweat from his eyes as he helped fortify the Union position on Cemetery Ridge. The relative quiet of the morning was unnerving after yesterday's chaos. "What are they waiting for?" he muttered.

William's unit moved into position near the base of a rocky hill. The men called it Little Round Top. "Looks like we're going around their flank," his sergeant explained. William nodded, a mixture of anticipation and dread building in his stomach.

General Meade rode along the Union line, inspecting defenses. His eyes kept drifting to the rocky hill at the end of the line - Little Round Top. It was exposed, vulnerable. "Send a brigade to secure that hill," he ordered. "It could be the key to our entire position." As he spoke, he remembered a lesson from his West Point days about the importance of high ground in defensive strategy.

July 2, 1863 - Late Afternoon

The sound of gunfire erupted from the Union left. Thomas's unit was quickly moved to reinforce the line. As they marched, he saw a group of soldiers racing up the slope of Little Round Top. "Double-quick, boys!" an officer shouted. "The Rebs are trying to turn our flank!"

William gasped for breath as he charged up the steep, rocky slope. The hill had seemed empty just moments ago, but now blue-coated soldiers appeared at the summit, firing down at them. He saw men falling around him but pressed on, the Confederate battle cry ringing in his ears.

Meade received reports of the assault on Little Round Top with growing concern. He'd sent the 20th Maine to hold the hill, but would it be enough? He dispatched riders with orders to reinforce the position at all costs. "If we lose that hill, we lose the battle," he told his staff, his usually calm demeanor showing signs of strain.

Thomas found himself on the crest of Little Round Top, part of a hastily formed line. The air was thick with smoke and the cries of wounded men. He fired his rifle again and again at the advancing Confederates. "Hold the line!" he heard someone shout. "For God's sake, hold the line!"

William had never known such exhaustion or terror. They'd almost reached the top, but the Union line held firm. He watched in horror as his friend beside him crumpled, a bullet in his chest. How many charges had they made now? He'd lost count. As he reloaded his rifle, he wondered how much longer they could keep this up.

July 2, 1863 - Evening

As darkness fell, Meade received word that Little Round Top had held. He closed his eyes briefly, offering a silent prayer of thanks. But there was no time for relief—reports were coming in of a massive assault on the Union center. "Redirect reserves to Cemetery Ridge," he ordered, his mind already racing ahead to the next crisis.

Thomas slumped against a boulder, his muscles aching, his ears ringing from hours of combat. They'd held the hill, but at a terrible cost. As he looked out over the battlefield, littered with bodies in blue and gray, he wondered how many more days of this hell they would have to endure.

William stumbled back down the blood-soaked slope of Little Round Top, part of the battered remnant of his unit. They'd given their all, but it hadn't been enough. As he collapsed into an exhausted sleep, his last thoughts were of home, so far away from this Pennsylvania hillside.

July 3, 1863 - Dawn

As the sun rose on the third day of battle, neither Thomas nor William could know that they were about to witness the most famous charge in American military history. On Cemetery Ridge and Seminary Ridge, two armies steeled themselves for what would be the decisive moment of the Battle of Gettysburg...

July 3, 1863 - Morning

Thomas helped redistribute ammunition along the Union line on Cemetery Ridge. The air was thick with tension. "Something big's coming," he overheard an officer say. "Lee's gonna try to break our center."

William sat cleaning his rifle, his hands shaking slightly. Rumors spread through the Confederate camps like wildfire. "We're going to hit them head-on," his sergeant explained. "One big push to break their line." William nodded, trying to quell the fear rising in his chest.

General Meade studied his maps intently. Lee had probed both flanks; logic dictated the next assault would come at the center. "Strengthen our position on Cemetery Ridge," he ordered. "Every available man and gun." As he issued the command, Meade reflected on the defensive tactics he'd learned at West Point, praying they would be enough.

July 3, 1863 - Early Afternoon

A deafening roar shattered the uneasy calm. Thomas ducked instinctively as Confederate artillery opened up, hundreds of guns firing in unison. "Here it comes, boys!" someone shouted. For nearly two hours, Thomas huddled behind the stone wall as shells screamed overhead.

William watched in awe as the greatest Confederate bombardment of the war rained down on the Union lines. The noise was incredible, the earth itself seeming to shake. "That'll soften them up," his lieutenant said confidently. But as the barrage continued, William couldn't shake a growing sense of dread.

Meade remained outwardly calm as shells exploded around his headquarters. "Hold your fire," he instructed his artillery commanders. "Wait until their infantry advances." It was a gamble, but one his years of military experience told him was necessary. They would need every round to repel the assault he knew was coming.

July 3, 1863 - Mid-Afternoon

The bombardment ceased, and an eerie silence fell over the battlefield. Thomas peered over the wall and felt his blood run cold. Across the open field, nearly a mile wide, an enormous line of Confederate soldiers was advancing. "Mother of God," he whispered.

William marched forward with Pickett's division, part of a line nearly a mile long. The open ground before them seemed endless, the Union position an impregnable fortress. Every step felt like it might be his last. Yet still they advanced, flags flying, towards the distant ridge.

"Withhold your fire," Meade ordered as the Confederate line came into range. "Let them come to us." He watched the advance with a mixture of admiration and sorrow. So many brave men, marching to their doom. But there could be no hesitation. The fate of the nation hung in the balance.

Thomas's world exploded into chaos as the Union line erupted in flame and smoke. He fired again and again, the heat of his rifle barrel burning his hands. The Confederate line staggered under the onslaught but kept coming. "Hold steady, boys!" he heard above the din. "Pour it into 'em!"

The world became a nightmare of smoke, screams, and death. William saw men falling all around him, torn apart by cannon fire and bullets. Yet somehow he kept moving forward, caught up in the tide of the advance. They were so close now, he could see the eyes of the Union defenders.

July 3, 1863 - Late Afternoon

Meade watched intently as the Confederate assault reached its climax. "Reinforce the center!" he commanded, committing his reserves. As the fighting reached its peak, he allowed himself a moment of reflection. All his years of training, all his military experience, had led to this moment.

Thomas grappled hand-to-hand with the Confederates who'd reached the wall. It was a brutal, desperate struggle. He saw the Union line waver, but then more men rushed in to plug the gaps. Slowly, inexorably, the Confederate attack began to falter.

William found himself at the Union wall, not knowing how he'd survived to reach it. But they were too few. As he looked back, he saw the magnificent charge had disintegrated into a chaotic retreat. "Fall back!" someone was shouting. "Every man for himself!" With a heavy heart, William turned and ran.

July 3, 1863 - Evening

As the sun set on Gettysburg, Thomas slumped against the blood-stained stone wall. They had held, but at a terrible cost. The field before Cemetery Ridge was carpeted with bodies in blue and gray. The moans of the wounded filled the air.

William stumbled back to the Confederate lines, one of the lucky few to return. As the magnitude of the defeat sank in, he felt a profound sense of loss. Not just for the friends he'd seen fall, but for the cause they'd fought for. Somehow, he knew, this day had decided far more than a single battle.

General Meade rode along the Union line, surveying the aftermath of the repulsed assault. They had won a great victory, but he felt no elation, only a deep weariness. As he considered the massive casualties on both sides, he remembered something he'd written in his West Point yearbook so long ago: "May we meet again on fields of glory." The fields of Gettysburg had certainly brought glory, but at what terrible cost?

Chapter 35

Four Days of Fire

The New York Draft Riots, July 1863

From the diary of Patrick O'Brien, Irish immigrant and laborer:

July 13, 1863

They said we'd have a lottery today, to choose who'd be sent off to die in this rich man's war. But we showed 'em. At dawn, we marched on the draft office on Third Avenue. Bricks flew, windows shattered. The damn wheel they use to pick names? We smashed it to kindling.

It ain't right, what they're doing. Three hundred dollars to buy your way out? Might as well be asking for the moon. And for what? To free the Negroes who'll come take our jobs? To hell with that, I say.

The streets are ours now. Them rich folk better watch out. They started this fire, now they're gonna burn.

Letter from Samuel Turner, free Black resident of Five Points, to his brother in Boston:

July 14, 1863

Dear James,

I pray this letter finds you well. New York has descended into madness. Yesterday, a mob attacked the Colored Orphan Asylum on Fifth Avenue. They set it ablaze, James. Children fled for their lives.

Now, gangs roam the streets, attacking any Black person they see. We've barricaded ourselves in our home. Sarah wanted to flee the city, but where would we go? This is our home, though right now it feels more like a battleground.

They say this is about the draft, but we know better. This is hate, plain and simple. The war to end slavery has brought all the poison to the surface.

Stay safe, brother. I fear this is far from over.

Excerpt from the journal of Police Commissioner Thomas Acton:

July 15, 1863

Third day of riots. City in chaos. Police overwhelmed, many injured. Sent urgent request to War Department for troops.

Mob growing bolder. Attacked wealthy homes on Lexington Avenue. Looted Brooks Brothers. Attempted to storm New York Times office—Henry Raymond and his staff drove them off with Gatling guns.

Most disturbing: lynchings reported. Several Black men hanged by mobs. God help us all.

Must restore order. But how? With what forces? Every hour brings new fires, new violence.

Telegram from Major General John E. Wool to Secretary of War Edwin Stanton:

JULY 16, 1863
WASHINGTON, D.C.

RIOTS LARGELY SUPPRESSED STOP FEDERAL TROOPS AND MILITIA REGIMENTS DEPLOYED THROUGHOUT CITY STOP ESTIMATE 120 CIVILIANS DEAD STOP OVER 2000 INJURED STOP PROPERTY DAMAGE EXTENSIVE STOP REQUEST ADDITIONAL FORCES TO MAINTAIN ORDER STOP

From the journal of Private Michael Collins, 7th New York State Militia:

July 16, 1863

Never thought I'd be fighting in the streets of my own city. We arrived from Maryland yesterday, and God almighty, what a sight. New York's burning, and it's our own people doing it.

Today we cleared out a mob on Second Avenue. They came at us with bricks and clubs, screaming about the draft and the rich man's war. Had to fix bayonets. The sound of steel entering flesh...Jesus, Mary, and Joseph, I'll never forget it.

These are our neighbors, our fellow New Yorkers. But orders are orders. We can't let the city fall to anarchy. Still, every time I level my rifle, I see faces I might've passed on the street a hundred times before.

They say we've mostly got it under control now. But at what cost? When this is over, how do we go back to being just New Yorkers again?

From the diary of Jacob Astor III, businessman:

July 17, 1863

The nightmare appears to be over. Four days of hell, but order is restored. From my window, I can see troops patrolling the streets. The fires are out, though the stench of smoke lingers.

They say over a hundred are dead, most of them rioters. Good riddance, I say. The draft will continue. It must. This war cannot be won without sacrifice—though I thank God my son's sacrifice will be financial rather than mortal.

New York will recover. We always do. But I fear the wounds opened these past days will be slow to heal.

Letter from Alderman William Wilson to his sister in Albany:

July 30, 1863

Dear Martha,

It's been two weeks since the draft riots ended, and New York is still reeling. The physical damage is being repaired—buildings rebuilt, streets cleared—but the wounds to our city's soul will take far longer to heal.

In yesterday's council meeting, we grappled with the aftermath. How do we prevent this from happening again? Some call for harsher policing in immigrant neighborhoods. Others argue we must address the underlying inequities that sparked the unrest.

The racial violence was particularly disturbing. We've set up a relief fund for the Colored Orphan Asylum, but that feels woefully inadequate. How do we protect our Black citizens and assure them they're safe in their own city?

And then there's the draft itself. It will resume next month, but we're all holding our breath. Will the riots flare up again? Have we done enough to address people's fears and resentments?

I find myself lying awake at night, wondering if we could have prevented this somehow. If we in city government had seen the signs, could we have averted this tragedy?

New York has survived crisis before, and we'll survive this. But I fear we'll be a changed city. The veneer of civility has been stripped away, and we've seen the raw anger and fear beneath. How we address that will define us for years to come.

Give my love to the children. And Martha, be grateful you're in Albany. New York may be the greatest city in the Union, but these days, it's also the most troubled.

Your weary brother,

William

Chapter 36

Valor Recognized

The 54th Massachusetts After Fort Wagner, September 1863

September 5, 1863 - Morris Island, South Carolina

The remnants of the 54th Massachusetts stood at attention, their ranks thinned by the brutal assault on Fort Wagner less than two months prior. Colonel Edward N. Hallowell, still nursing his own wounds from that fateful day, surveyed the men before him. Their faces, etched with both pride and sorrow, told the story of their sacrifice.

"Men of the 54th," Hallowell began, his voice carrying across the assembled troops, "we gather here today not just as soldiers, but as men who have forever changed the course of this war and, indeed, the very fabric of our nation."

A murmur rippled through the ranks. Hallowell allowed himself a small smile before continuing.

"Your valor at Fort Wagner has echoed far beyond these shores. You have proven, beyond any doubt, the fighting spirit and courage of the colored soldier. And your actions have not gone unnoticed in the highest circles of our government."

Hallowell paused, reaching into his coat to withdraw an envelope.

"I have here a letter, men. A letter that I believe will mean more to you than any official commendation. It is from Mrs. Mary Todd Lincoln herself."

A collective gasp arose from the assembled soldiers. Sergeant William H. Carney, still recovering from the wounds he received while ensuring the American flag never touched the ground during the assault, leaned forward, his eyes wide.

"Mrs. Lincoln, having heard of your bravery from the President himself, has taken the extraordinary step of writing to us directly. With your permission, I shall read her words."

As Hallowell broke the seal on the envelope, a hush fell over the men. Even the distant boom of cannon fire seemed to fade away as he began to read:

"To the brave men of the 54th Massachusetts Volunteer Infantry Regiment,

I write to you today with a heart full of gratitude and admiration. News of your valor in the assault on Fort Wagner has reached Washington, and I assure you that your courage has not gone unnoticed or unappreciated.

My husband, the President, spoke to me at length about your regiment's charge. The fire in his eyes as he recounted your bravery was unlike anything I have seen in these long, dark years of war. He said to me, 'Mary, these men have done more for the cause of freedom in one night than a hundred speeches could ever accomplish.'

I must confess, there was a time when I, like many, harbored doubts about the capabilities of colored troops. Your actions at

Fort Wagner have put such doubts to rest forever. You have proven beyond question that bravery, loyalty, and love of country know no color.

My heart aches for the terrible losses you have suffered, particularly your valiant commander, Colonel Shaw. Please know that his sacrifice, and the sacrifice of all who fell that day, shall not be in vain. Your blood, shed on the ramparts of Fort Wagner, has consecrated the cause of liberty anew.

In the nights since hearing of your charge, I have found myself reflecting on the words of our Declaration of Independence—that all men are created equal. You, brave soldiers, have given new meaning to those words. You have shown that equality must be earned not just in legislative halls, but on the field of battle as well.

I am told that your regiment's motto is 'Liberty, Loyalty, and Unity.' Know that you have embodied these virtues in the truest sense, and in doing so, you have made your nation proud.

May God bless and keep you all.

With deepest respect and gratitude,

Mary Todd Lincoln"

As Colonel Hallowell folded the letter, a profound silence fell over the assembled men. Then, slowly, a murmur began to build, swelling into a cheer that echoed across Morris Island.

Sergeant Carney, tears glistening in his eyes, straightened to his full height. "Three cheers for Mrs. Lincoln!" he called out. The response was deafening.

As the cheers faded, Colonel Hallowell raised his hand for silence. "Men of the 54th," he said, his voice thick with emotion, "let this letter serve as a reminder of what we fight for. Not just for ourselves, but for generations yet unborn. Our struggle is far from over, but take pride in knowing that your courage has lit a flame that cannot be extinguished. Dismissed."

As the men dispersed, there was a new spring in their step, a fresh determination in their eyes. They had proven themselves in battle, and now they had been recognized by the highest powers in the land. The 54th Massachusetts had indeed changed the course of the war, and perhaps, the course of history itself.

Chapter 37

The Weight of Words

Lincoln Crafts the Gettysburg Address, November 1863

November 17, 1863 - The White House, Washington D.C.

The invitation sits on my desk, its official seal gleaming in the lamplight. Dedicate the cemetery at Gettysburg? My first instinct is to decline. I'm no orator like Edward Everett, who's set to give the main speech. What could I, Abraham Lincoln, possibly add?

But as I gaze out the window at the Washington night, something stirs within me. Gettysburg. The turning point of this bloody war. Perhaps this is an opportunity not just to honor the dead, but to remind the living what we're fighting for.

I reach for a fresh sheet of paper. The words don't come easily at first. How do you capture the magnitude of such sacrifice in mere sentences? I think of the soldiers I've visited in field hospitals, of the telegrams announcing casualties that cross my desk daily. This speech must be more than a eulogy; it must be a renewal of purpose.

"Four score and seven years ago," I write, then pause. Yes, tie it back to the founding of our nation. Remind them of the principles we're struggling to uphold...

The candle burns low as I wrestle with each word, each phrase. This speech must be brief—the people have heard enough long-winded orations—but it must also resonate. I find myself returning to the ideas of rebirth, of a nation conceived in liberty but now in the throes of a great test.

I crumple another draft, frustrated. How to convey the magnitude of our loss while instilling hope for the future? The faces of grieving mothers and widows flash through my mind. For them, this war is not about grand ideals but about empty chairs at dinner tables.

"...that these dead shall not have died in vain," I write, the words flowing more freely now. Yes, we owe it to the fallen to ensure their sacrifice leads to a better nation.

Dawn breaks as I finally set down my pen, exhausted but satisfied. The speech is short—some might say too short for such an occasion—but every word carries the weight of our struggle.

As I prepare for the journey to Gettysburg, doubt creeps in. Will the people understand what I'm trying to convey? Will these words bring comfort, or will they ring hollow in the face of such immense loss?

The train ride to Pennsylvania is somber. I notice the still-visible scars of battle on the landscape, a stark reminder of the cost of this war. In my pocket, the speech feels like a living thing, each carefully chosen word humming with potential energy.

As we approach the makeshift podium on that overcast November day, the magnitude of the moment washes over me. Before me lie thousands of fresh graves, each representing a life given for the cause of Union and liberty. The crowd waits, expectant.

I take a deep breath, unfolding the paper that contains what I hope will be more than just words, but a renewed call to action for a wounded nation.

And so I begin:

"Four score and seven years ago our fathers brought forth, upon this continent, a new nation, conceived in Liberty, and dedicated to the proposition that all men are created equal.

Now we are engaged in a great civil war, testing whether that nation, or any nation so conceived, and so dedicated, can long endure..."

Chapter 38

A Bittersweet Yuletide

Christmas 1863 with Elias and Jeremiah

Boston, Massachusetts - December 23, 1863

Elias Merriweather stood in his general store, surveying the sparse shelves. The war had made many items scarce, but he'd managed to secure a few luxuries for the holidays. As he arranged a display of oranges—exorbitantly priced but a Christmas tradition—the bell over the door jingled.

"Pa! Look what I found!" His daughter Emily burst in, waving a newspaper. "It's the full text of Mr. Lincoln's speech at Gettysburg. Can we read it tonight?"

Elias smiled, remembering the night they'd first read about the address. "Of course, dear. We'll read it after supper."

As Emily skipped out, Elias's wife Sarah entered, her face drawn with worry. "Any word from Thomas?" she asked.

Elias shook his head. Their son had been with Grant's army at Chattanooga. "No, but no news is good news, remember?"

Sarah nodded, but her eyes glistened with unshed tears. "It's not the Christmas I'd hoped for."

Elias put his arm around her. "I know, dear. But we have much to be thankful for. And who knows? Maybe we'll get a Christmas miracle."

****

Outside Atlanta, Georgia - December 24, 1863

Jeremiah Calhoun sat on his porch, whittling a small wooden horse. It would be William's only Christmas gift, if the package made it through to Virginia. His younger son James approached, a letter in hand.

"It's from Will, Pa," James said, his voice a mix of excitement and apprehension.

Jeremiah took the letter with trembling hands. As he read, a small smile crossed his weathered face. "He's alive and well," he announced. "Says he'll be thinking of us on Christmas Day."

Inside, Mary Calhoun stirred a pot of soup made from the last of their garden's winter vegetables. "At least we'll have a warm meal," she said, trying to sound cheerful.

Jeremiah nodded, his mind on the contents of William's letter. His son had mentioned Lincoln's speech at Gettysburg, describing how even some Confederate soldiers had grudgingly admired its eloquence.

"'Four score and seven years ago,'" Jeremiah muttered. "Fancy words won't change the fact that they're invading our land."

"What was that, dear?" Mary called from the kitchen.

"Nothing," Jeremiah replied. "Just thinking about Will."

As night fell, the Calhoun family gathered around their small table. "Let us give thanks," Jeremiah began, "for what little we have, and pray for better days ahead."

****

Boston - Christmas Morning

The Merriweathers were awakened by a pounding on their door. Elias rushed downstairs, fearing bad news. Instead, he found a grinning Thomas on the doorstep, home on unexpected leave.

As the family embraced, laughing and crying, Elias thought of Lincoln's words: "It is for us the living, rather, to be dedicated here to the unfinished work which they who fought here have thus far so nobly advanced."

Looking at his son, alive and whole, Elias silently vowed to do whatever he could to support that unfinished work, to ensure that Thomas's sacrifices—and those of so many others—would not be in vain.

****

Outside Atlanta - Christmas Morning

The Calhouns rose early, exchanging the few small gifts they'd managed to prepare. As Rebecca exclaimed over a new hair ribbon made from one of Mary's old dresses, a commotion arose outside.

Jeremiah opened the door to find his neighbors, the Wilsons, standing there with baskets of food. "We all pitched in," Mrs. Wilson explained. "No one should go hungry on Christmas."

Overwhelmed by this act of generosity, Jeremiah invited them in. As they shared the unexpected feast, he found himself thinking again of Lincoln's words. The war had brought such suffering, but it had also shown the strength of their community.

"We're all in this together," Jeremiah thought, watching his family and neighbors laugh and talk. "And together, somehow, we'll see it through."

1864

Chapter 39

A New Strategy

Grant Briefs Lincoln, March 1864

The White House - March 8, 1864

The grandfather clock in the corner of President Lincoln's office ticked steadily, marking the passage of time as General Ulysses S. Grant spread a large map across the President's desk. Lincoln leaned forward, his lanky frame hunched over the document, eyes fixed on the terrain between Washington and Richmond.

"Mr. President," Grant began, his voice gravelly from years of cigar smoke, "what I propose is a coordinated effort across all theaters of the war. But the main thrust will be here, in Virginia."

Lincoln nodded, his deep-set eyes studying Grant's face. "Go on, General. You have my full attention."

Grant's stubby finger traced a line from Washington towards Richmond. "We'll advance with the Army of the Potomac, engaging Lee's forces directly. But unlike previous campaigns, we won't retreat if we meet setbacks. We'll keep pressing forward, flanking and maneuvering as needed."

"And if Lee blocks you?" Lincoln asked, his voice tinged with the weariness of years of false starts and defeats. He couldn't help but think of McClellan's hesitation, Burnside's blunders at Fredericksburg, Hooker's defeat at Chancellorsville.

A grim smile played at the corners of Grant's mouth. "Then we fight, Mr. President. We fight until we win. Lee's army, not Richmond, is our true objective. We destroy that army, the war ends."

Lincoln straightened, stroking his beard thoughtfully. "It will be costly, General. The people are tired of long casualty lists." He paused, his eyes clouding with the memory of thousands of telegrams bearing news of death and injury. "And I face re-election this year. The peace Democrats are gaining ground."

"It will be costly, sir," Grant agreed, his face set with determination. "But it's the quickest way to end this war. We have the resources to sustain losses. The Confederacy doesn't. It's simple arithmetic."

The President was quiet for a long moment, his eyes distant. Lincoln wrestled with the weight of his decision. How many more lives would this strategy claim? Could the Union - could he - bear the cost of Grant's relentless approach? Yet, if it could end the war...

When he spoke, his voice was soft but firm. "Your plan is a departure from what we've tried before, General. No retreat, constant pressure...it's bold. Risky. But perhaps that's what we need." He sighed heavily. "Very well, General Grant. You have my approval. When do you propose to begin?"

Grant rolled up the map with a sense of finality. "We'll move out in May, sir. And we won't stop until this war is won."

As Grant turned to leave, Lincoln called out, "General?" Grant paused at the door. "God go with you," the President said. Then, almost to himself, he added, "And may He forgive us for what must be done."

Grant nodded once, then strode out, leaving Lincoln alone with the weight of the decision they had just made. The tick of the grandfather clock seemed to grow louder, counting down to the brutal campaign that lay ahead. Lincoln turned to the window, gazing out at the city beyond. In his mind's eye, he could already see the casualty lists, the grieving families, the political storms to come. But he also saw a glimmer of hope—a chance, at last, to end this terrible war.

"The stakes have never been higher," he murmured to the empty room. "For the Union, for freedom, for my presidency...May we prove equal to the task."

Chapter 40

The New York Tribune, August 1864

THE NEW YORK TRIBUNE
August 15, 1864

GRANT'S CAMPAIGN: A COSTLY PATH TO RICH-
MOND'S DOORSTEP

By Horace Greeley, Editor-in-Chief

After three months of relentless fighting, General Ulysses S. Grant's Overland Campaign has brought the Union Army to the gates of Richmond, albeit at a staggering cost in lives and resources.

Beginning on May 4, Grant's forces have engaged in a series of brutal battles against General Robert E. Lee's Army of Northern Virginia. The engagements at the Wilderness (May 5-7), Spotsylvania Court House (May 8-21), and Cold Harbor (May 31-June 12) have resulted in unprecedented casualties, with estimates suggesting over 50,000 Union soldiers killed, wounded, or missing. Confederate losses, while lower, are estimated at 32,000—a number the South can ill afford.

Despite these losses, Grant has achieved what his predecessors could not: maintaining continuous pressure on Lee's army and driving it back to the Confederate capital. The Army of the Potomac now besieges Petersburg, a crucial supply hub for Richmond, as part of Grant's overall strategy to strangle the Confederacy's resources.

Critics argue that the cost in lives has been too high, dubbing Grant "The Butcher." Senator Benjamin Wade of Ohio remarked, "This war cannot be won by sacrificing an entire generation of young men." Supporters, however, point out that Lee's army has suffered losses it cannot replace, while Grant continues to receive reinforcements.

The campaign has taken its toll on Northern morale, with war weariness growing among civilians. The upcoming presidential election has intensified debate over the war's conduct, with some calling for a negotiated peace. However, recent naval victories, including Admiral Farragut's success at Mobile Bay on August 5, have provided a boost to Union spirits.

President Lincoln, when asked about the campaign's progress, stated, "General Grant has the bear by the hind leg, and he's not letting go."

As summer wanes, the nation watches with bated breath. Will Grant's strategy of attrition finally bring this bloody conflict to an end, or will Lee find a way to break the iron grip now tightening around the Confederacy's throat?

Only time will tell, but one thing is certain: the war has entered a new and perhaps final phase, one that may determine the fate of our divided nation.

Chapter 41

Blood on the Bluffs

The Fort Pillow Investigation, May 1864

Washington, D.C. - May 5, 1864

The somber faces of the Joint Committee on the Conduct of the War reflected the gravity of the report before them. Established by Congress in December 1861 to oversee the conduct of the war effort, the committee had investigated numerous military matters, but none as horrifying as what they were about to discuss.

Senator Benjamin Wade of Ohio, the committee chairman, cleared his throat and began to read:

"Gentlemen, we are gathered here today to present our findings on the incident at Fort Pillow, Tennessee. What we have uncovered is nothing short of an atrocity that shakes the very foundations of civilized warfare."

A murmur rippled through the assembled congressmen. Wade continued, his voice growing stronger:

"On April 12, 1864, Confederate forces under the command of General Nathan Bedford Forrest attacked Fort Pillow. While the fort held little strategic value, its garrison of almost 600 men, nearly half of them former slaves, made it a tempting target. What followed was not battle, but butchery. Our investigation has found evidence of the most shocking brutality, particularly directed at colored troops who had surrendered.

Wade paused, his eyes scanning the room. "I warn you, gentlemen, the testimony we are about to present is not for the faint of heart."

He nodded to the clerk, who began to read from the first survivor's account:

"I saw the Rebels shoot down our men who had thrown down their arms and begged for their lives. They pulled some of the Negro soldiers out of the hospital and shot them down in cold blood. I saw them burn huts and tents with wounded soldiers still inside..."

As the clerk's voice droned on, detailing the horrors witnessed at Fort Pillow, several committee members paled visibly. Representative Daniel Gooch of Massachusetts interjected:

"Mr. Chairman, are we certain of the veracity of these accounts? The claims seem almost too barbaric to be believed."

Wade's expression hardened. "We have corroborating testimony from multiple survivors, both white and colored. But let us continue with the evidence, and you may judge for yourself."

He gestured for the clerk to proceed. As the gruesome details of the massacre unfolded, it became clear to all present that the Fort Pillow incident would forever change the nature of the war.

The clerk turned to the next page. "We shall now hear the testimony of Sergeant Archie Kerney, 6th U.S. Colored Heavy Artillery."

Sergeant Archie Kerney's testimony hung in the air, his words painting a vivid and horrifying picture:

"After we surrendered, they shot us down like dogs. I saw them kill wounded men, pleading for mercy. They set fire to our hospital with injured men still inside. The screams...I'll never forget those screams."

Senator Charles Sumner of Massachusetts, his face ashen, interrupted. "And what of General Forrest? Was he present during these...atrocities?"

The clerk shuffled through the papers. "According to multiple accounts, General Forrest was indeed present. Private Samuel Caldwell testified:

'I saw General Forrest shoot a Negro soldier point-blank who was carrying a wounded officer off the field. When Forrest saw the man was still breathing, he turned to one of his men and said, "If he ain't dead, shoot him again." And they did.'"

A collective gasp echoed through the chamber. Representative Gooch, still skeptical, spoke up again. "Surely there must be some explanation. Perhaps the fog of war..."

Wade cut him off sharply. "The fog of war does not explain the systematic execution of surrendered soldiers, Representative. But let us continue. We have here a report on the casualties."

The clerk read out the grim statistics: "Of the 600 Union troops present, nearly 300 were killed. The Confederate forces suffered fewer than 100 casualties. Most tellingly, while only 20% of white Union soldiers were killed, over 60% of the colored troops perished."

Senator Wade's voice was thick with emotion as he added, "It is clear, gentlemen, that this was no ordinary battle. This was a massacre, one that targeted colored troops with particular savagery."

The room fell silent as the weight of the evidence sank in. Finally, Representative George Julian of Indiana spoke. "What are we to do with this information? Surely we cannot allow such barbarity to go unanswered."

Wade nodded grimly. "Indeed, we cannot. This committee recommends the following actions:

First, that this report be made public, so that the nation may know the true face of this rebellion.

Second, that colored troops be afforded equal protection and treatment as white soldiers, both in battle and as prisoners of war.

Third, that the Confederate leadership be held accountable for these war crimes.

And finally, that we use every means at our disposal to bring this war to a swift conclusion, lest more atrocities of this nature occur."

As the committee members began to discuss the recommendations, the clerk quietly added one final piece of testimony to the record. It was from a Confederate soldier who had participated in the attack:

"I saw things that day that no man should see, and did things no man should do. May God forgive us all."

Senator Wade cleared his throat. "Let the record show that this incident occurred just one week after the U.S. Senate passed the 13th Amendment abolishing slavery. The juxtaposition of these events only underscores the crucial nature of our struggle."

****

The Fort Pillow Massacre would indeed change the nature of the war. It would harden Northern resolve, intensify the fight for equal treatment of colored troops, and leave a lasting stain on the Confederate cause. As the committee adjourned, each member knew that the war had entered a new, more terrible phase—one where the lines between combat and cruelty had become terrifyingly blurred.

Chapter 42

Hell on Earth

Voices from Andersonville, August 1864

August 15, 1864 - Camp Sumter (Andersonville Prison), Georgia

The Georgia sun beat down mercilessly on Camp Sumter, turning the overcrowded prison into a furnace of misery. Private John Emerson, once a robust farm boy from Ohio, now a skeletal shadow of his former self, leaned against the remnants of a crude shelter. His eyes, sunken and feverish, scanned the sea of suffering around him.

"Water," croaked a voice beside him. "John, please... water."

John turned to his friend, Sergeant William Hayes, a Massachusetts schoolteacher who'd enlisted with dreams of adventure. Those dreams had died here in this hellhole they called Andersonville.

"Wish I had some to give you, Will," John replied, his voice barely above a whisper. "The creek's more poison than water these days."

Will nodded weakly, his parched lips cracking as he tried to speak again. "How...how many today?"

John didn't need to ask what he meant. Every morning, they counted the dead. It had become a grim ritual, a way to mark the passage of time in this timeless purgatory.

"Twenty-three in our section alone," John answered, his tone flat. Emotion was a luxury they could no longer afford. "Saw them carting off more from the other side of the camp. Cholera's spreading fast."

It was the only marker of time they had left—the grim morning ritual of counting and carting away the dead. There were no work details, no roll calls, nothing to differentiate one hellish day from the next. Just the endless cycle of suffering, broken only by the occasional fight over a scrap of food or the arrival of new prisoners.

The stench of death and decay hung heavily in the air, mingling with the foul odor of the open sewer that ran through the center of the camp. Men, packed together like cattle, moved listlessly or lay where they fell, too weak to stand.

John had overheard a guard mention that the camp was built for 10,000 men. Now, in the sweltering August heat, over 30,000 souls were crammed into the 26-acre pen. Every square foot of ground seemed occupied by a body, living or dead.

"Remember when we first got here?" Will asked, a hint of bitter irony in his voice. "Thought it couldn't get worse than Belle Isle."

John let out a humorless chuckle. "Guess the Rebs proved us wrong on that count." He paused, trying to calculate the days. "How long's it been now? Three months? Four? Hard to believe we once thought this was just a temporary stop before a prisoner exchange."

A commotion near the gate drew their attention. New prisoners were being marched in, their faces a mix of fear and defiance. John watched as the newcomers' eyes widened in horror at the sight that greeted them.

"Poor bastards," he muttered. "They've no idea what they're in for."

Will's gaze drifted to the "deadline," the wooden railing that marked the no-man's land near the stockade walls. "Saw another one shot yesterday. Kid couldn't have been more than sixteen. Reached under for a scrap of moldy bread."

John nodded grimly. The guards' brutality was as much a part of Andersonville as the lice that infested their ragged uniforms.

"You hear about Captain Wirz's latest order?" John asked, changing the subject. "No more trading with the guards. Says he'll shoot any man caught doing it."

Will closed his eyes, a single tear cutting a path through the grime on his cheek. "We're going to die here, aren't we, John?"

John wanted to offer words of hope, to say that rescue was coming, that the war would end, that they'd see home again. But lies stuck in his throat. Instead, he placed a hand on his friend's bony shoulder.

"If we do," he said softly, "we'll do it as Union men. We'll do it with honor."

As the sun began to set, casting long shadows across the desolate camp, John and Will fell into a silence born of exhaustion and despair. Around them, thirty thousand souls endured, each lost in their own private hell. Andersonville, in all its horror, stood as a testament to the depths of human cruelty and the heights of human endurance.

In the fading light, a whisper passed through the camp like a ghost—a rumor of Sherman's army advancing, of impending liberation. But for John, Will, and countless others, such hopes seemed as distant and unreachable as the stars beginning to appear in the darkening Georgia sky.

Chapter 43

The Road to Atlanta

Dueling Commanders, May – September 1864

The Atlanta Campaign, lasting from May to September 1864, was a crucial series of battles in the Western Theater of the Civil War. Its outcome would have far-reaching consequences for both the military situation and the upcoming presidential election in the North. The following entries from the commanding generals on both sides offer a unique insight into this pivotal campaign.

****

May 7, 1864 -- General William T. Sherman

The campaign begins. My army of 100,000 men moves south from Chattanooga today. Our objective: Joe Johnston's army and the vital rail hub of Atlanta. The terrain favors Johnston—all mountains and rivers. But we have numbers and supplies on our side. I've told Grant I'll "make Georgia howl." Time to make good on that promise. With each step south, we tighten the noose around the Confederacy's neck. Atlanta's fall could well mean the end of this bloody war.

May 8, 1864 -- General Joseph E. Johnston

Sherman's juggernaut is on the move. I have but 50,000 men to oppose him, yet I'm confident in our defensive position at Rocky Face Ridge. Let Sherman dash himself against our fortifications. We'll bleed him dry before he ever sees Atlanta. Our men are in high spirits, ready to defend their homeland. Sherman may have numbers, but we have determination and the advantage of fighting on our own soil.

May 15, 1864 - Sherman

Johnston's no fool. He slipped away from Rocky Face Ridge before I could pin him down. Now he's dug in at Resaca. No matter. I'll keep pressing, keep flanking. This war of maneuver suits me fine. Every mile south is a victory. We've suffered about 6,000 casualties so far, but Johnston's losses are proportionally higher. This war of attrition favors us in the long run.

May 20, 1864 - Johnston

We've fallen back again, this time to Allatoona Pass. Sherman's relentless pressure and flanking moves are testing us, but I won't give him the decisive battle he seeks. Let him stretch his supply lines. Time and terrain are on our side. The men grumble about retreating, but I must think of the bigger picture. Every day we delay Sherman is a day gained for our cause.

May 25, 1864 - Lieutenant Thomas Parker, 20th Tennessee Infantry

The constant marching is wearing us down. We've been digging trenches one day only to abandon them the next. Some of the men wonder why we don't stand and fight, but I trust General Johnston. He's keeping us alive, and that's no small feat against Sherman's hordes.

June 10, 1864 - Sherman

Damn this rain! We're bogged down near Marietta, and Johnston's dug in on Kennesaw Mountain. My men are grumbling about the constant marching and skirmishing. Maybe it's time for a direct assault, show them we can still fight head-on. We've advanced nearly 100 miles in a month, but at what cost? Over 20,000 casualties, and Atlanta still seems so far away.

June 27, 1864 - Johnston

Sherman finally obliged us with a frontal attack on Kennesaw Mountain. We bloodied his nose properly. Yet I fear it's only a matter of time before he resumes his flanking maneuvers. The army's morale is high, but how long can we keep retreating? The victory has boosted spirits, but I can see the strain on the men's faces. We've lost nearly 10,000 soldiers since this campaign began. How much longer can we hold out?

July 17, 1864 - Sherman

Johnston's gone, replaced by Hood. Davis must be desperate. Hood's a fighter, not a defender like Johnston. This might be the opening we need. Atlanta is within our grasp. The change in command is a gift. Hood's aggressive nature will play right into our hands.

July 20, 1864 -- General John Bell Hood

I will not retreat anymore. Today we strike back, hit Sherman before he can surround Atlanta. My men are eager for the offensive. We'll show these Yankees what Southern steel can do. The change in strategy has reinvigorated the army. Johnston's caution has been replaced by a new fighting spirit. Atlanta will not fall without a fight.

July 22, 1864 - Sherman

Hood's a madman. Two days of furious assaults have cost him dearly. My line bent but didn't break. Now Atlanta lies open before us. Yet I'm uneasy. Urban fighting could be costly. Perhaps there's another way...Hood's attacks have cost him over 20,000 men. Our losses are half that. This war of attrition is swinging decisively in our favor.

July 25, 1864 - Hood

Our attacks have failed to dislodge Sherman, and the cost has been terrible. But I cannot, will not, give up Atlanta without a fight. As long as we hold the city, we have hope. I must find a way to break Sherman's grip. The men's morale is wavering. They've lost confidence in me, I fear. But I must press on. To retreat now would doom us all.

August 25, 1864 - Sherman

A bold stroke: we've pulled back from Atlanta, swinging south to cut Hood's supply lines. He'll have to come out and fight or starve in the city. Either way, Atlanta will fall. The end is near. This maneuver is risky, but it's the key to taking Atlanta without a costly direct assault. Hood's aggression will be his undoing.

September 1, 1864 - Hood

It's over. We must abandon Atlanta or be trapped. As I write this, the city burns behind me, our supplies and munitions put to the torch. This is a dark day for the Confederacy, but the war is not yet lost. We will fight on. The decision to burn our own supplies tears at my heart, but we cannot let them fall into enemy hands. May God forgive me for this necessary act.

September 3, 1864 - Sherman

Atlanta is ours. The telegram has gone to Washington: "Atlanta is ours, and fairly won." This victory may well secure Lincoln's re-election and with it, the final triumph of our cause. But my work is not done. I look east, to the sea, and consider our next move. The campaign has cost us dearly—over 30,000 casualties. But the prize is worth it. The Confederacy's industrial heart is now in Union hands. The end of this war is finally in sight.

Chapter 44

A Nation Divided

The Great Debate of 1864

October 15, 1864 - Boston, Massachusetts

The bell over the door of Merriweather's General Store jingled as Elias began to close up for the evening. He looked up to see James Hawthorne, his oldest friend and owner of the haberdashery next door, striding in with a newspaper clutched in his hand.

"Elias, my friend," James called out, his face flushed with excitement, "have you seen the latest? McClellan's gaining ground in the polls!"

Elias sighed, setting aside the ledger he'd been balancing. "James, you know I don't hold with your views on the election. Lincoln's our best hope for seeing this war through."

James pulled up a stool to the counter, spreading the newspaper out between them. "See here," he pointed to a headline, "McClellan promises peace negotiations. Isn't it time we ended this bloody conflict?"

Elias frowned. "You're talking about the same McClellan who Lincoln removed from command for his reluctance to engage the enemy. Now he wants to negotiate with them?"

James countered, "And Lincoln? He was a one-term congress-man before becoming president. At least McClellan has military experience."

"That's true," Elias admitted, "but Lincoln's grown into the role. He's guided us through the darkest days of this war."

A few lingering customers turned to listen, drawn by the passion in the shopkeepers' voices.

James leaned in, his tone earnest. "Elias, we've been friends for thirty years. You know I'm no Confederate sympathizer. But this war...it's tearing us apart. The dead and wounded return daily. Families are broken. For God's sake, even your Thomas—"

"Leave my boy out of this," Elias snapped, then took a deep breath. "I'm sorry, James. But that's precisely why we can't change course now. Thomas and thousands like him have sacrificed too much for us to turn back."

An older gentleman, a regular customer, stepped forward. "If I may, gentlemen. Mr. Merriweather speaks sense. Lincoln may not be perfect, but we can't afford to show weakness now."

"Weakness?" James scoffed. "Is it weak to seek peace? To end the bloodshed?"

As more customers gathered around, voicing their own opinions, Elias realized this impromptu debate was far from over. He reached for the coffee pot. It was going to be a long night.

"All right, James," Elias said, pouring two cups. "You want to do this? Let's do this properly. Make your case for McClellan, and I'll tell you why Lincoln deserves four more years."

James accepted the coffee with a nod, a glint of challenge in his eye. "You're on, old friend. But don't blame me when I change your vote."

As the two men settled in, their audience pulled up stools and crates, eager to witness this clash of ideas that mirrored the division gripping the nation.

James took a sip of coffee, gathering his thoughts. "Look, Elias, nobody's denying Lincoln's good intentions. But the fact is, this war has dragged on for over three years now. How many more must die before we admit it's a stalemate?"

Elias shook his head. "A stalemate? Have you forgotten Sherman's taking of Atlanta? Or Farragut's victory at Mobile Bay? We're making progress, James."

"At what cost?" James countered. "The Wilderness, Cold Harbor, Petersburg—the casualty lists grow longer with each battle. McClellan understands the toll this war is taking. He's a military man; he knows when to fight and when to negotiate."

A woman in the crowd spoke up. "My son died at Gettysburg. Are you saying his sacrifice was for nothing?"

James turned to her, his voice softening. "No, ma'am. I'm saying let's not add your other son to that list if we can help it."

Elias leaned forward. "James, I understand the desire for peace. We all want this war to end. But consider this: if we negotiate now, from a position of growing strength, what message does that send? That the Union can be broken if the secessionists just hold out long enough?"

"Elias has a point," the older gentleman chimed in. "We must see this through, or our grandchildren might face the same fight."

James wasn't backing down. "But at what point does the cure become worse than the disease? Lincoln's suspended habeas corpus, instituted a draft...Where does it end? McClellan would restore our civil liberties."

"Desperate times, desperate measures," Elias retorted. "Would you have us keep our hands tied while fighting for the very survival of our nation?"

A younger man in the crowd spoke up. "What about the slaves? If McClellan wins, what happens to emancipation?"

James hesitated, and Elias seized the opening. "Exactly. Lincoln's Emancipation Proclamation wasn't just a moral stand—it's a strategic one. It's undermined the Confederacy's economy and bolstered our own forces with colored troops. Would you undo all that?"

"The Proclamation only freed slaves in rebel states," James argued. "It was a war measure, not a moral crusade."

"Perhaps," Elias conceded, "but it's a start. And Lincoln's committed to seeing it through. Can McClellan say the same?"

The younger man spoke up again. "I heard that down South, they're watching our election closely. A cousin of mine who escaped from Richmond said the Confederates are hoping for a McClellan victory. They think he'll be easier to negotiate with."

James looked uncomfortable at this, while Elias seized on the point. "You see? Even the enemy knows that a vote for McClellan is a vote for a weakened Union."

As the debate raged on, customers chimed in with their own views. Some backed Elias, citing the need for stability and the fear that a change in leadership would be seen as weakness. Others sided with James, expressing war-weariness and concern over the conflict's mounting costs.

As the evening wore on, it became clear that neither Elias nor James would sway the other. But their passionate exchange had sparked a broader discussion, reflecting the nation's own struggle with these weighty issues.

Finally, as the clock struck ten, Elias held up his hands. "Well, James, I think we've talked ourselves hoarse, and I doubt either of us has changed the other's mind."

James nodded, a rueful smile on his face. "True enough, old friend. But I'll tell you what—let's make a wager. Loser buys the winner a bottle of that fine Kentucky bourbon we both favor."

Elias chuckled, extending his hand. "You're on. And no matter the outcome, the day after the election, we'll share that bottle and toast to the Union, whatever shape it may take."

As the impromptu audience began to disperse, still arguing amongst themselves, Elias and James shook hands. Their debate was a microcosm of the larger national conversation, a testament to the democracy they were fighting to preserve.

As Elias locked up the store, he couldn't shake the feeling that their debate tonight was being echoed in general stores, taverns, and homes across the North. The outcome of this election would determine not just the fate of the war, but the very future of the Union. Whether Lincoln's steady hand or McClellan's promise of peace would prevail was now up to the American people. In a few short weeks, the nation would make its choice, and history would be forever changed.

Chapter 45

The Die is Cast

Davis Contemplates Lincoln's Victory, November 1864

Richmond, Virginia - November 12, 1864

Jefferson Davis stood at the window of his study in the Confederate White House, a telegram clutched in his hand. The pale morning light did little to soften the hard lines of worry etched on his face.

"Mr. President?" his secretary inquired softly from the doorway.

Davis turned, his expression grim. "It's confirmed, Burton. Lincoln has indeed secured his second term."

As the secretary quietly withdrew, Davis sank into his chair, allowing himself a moment of unguarded contemplation. Lincoln's re-election was not unexpected, but the reality of it struck him like a physical blow.

"So, the North chooses to press on," he murmured to himself. "They reject McClellan's overtures of peace for Lincoln's promise of victory through devastation."

He picked up a report from General Lee, detailing the increasingly dire situation facing the Army of Northern Virginia. Supply shortages, dwindling manpower, the stranglehold of Grant's siege at Petersburg—all painted a bleak picture.

Yet, Davis refused to succumb to despair. He dipped his pen in ink and began to write, his resolve strengthening with each word:

"The re-election of Lincoln ensures the continuance of the war. The people of the North have chosen this path, but we shall show them the folly of their choice. Our cause is just, our determination unshakable.

"We must impress upon our citizens and soldiers that this is the darkest hour before the dawn. The enemy thinks to break us through attrition and devastation, but they underestimate the resilience of a people fighting for their very way of life.

"Our course is clear. We shall fight on, with every means at our disposal. Let Richmond be an example to every city, every town. We shall resist to the last man, the last bullet. For in our resistance lies our path to victory and independence."

Davis set down his pen, reading over his words. They were meant as much to bolster his own resolve as they were to rally the Confederate government and people.

A knock at the door interrupted his thoughts. "Enter," he called.

Secretary of State Judah Benjamin stepped in, his face grave. "Mr. President, I've just received word from Georgia. Sherman has left Atlanta and is marching eastward. We don't know his exact target."

Davis's jaw tightened. "With Lincoln re-elected, Sherman will only grow bolder. We must prepare our people for hard times ahead, Judah. But we must also show them that our cause is not lost. Draft a message to Governor Brown. Tell him to mobilize every able-bodied man to resist Sherman's advance."

Benjamin nodded. "And our overall strategy, sir? With Lincoln promising to continue the war until unconditional surrender..."

"We adapt," Davis said firmly. "We make every mile Sherman advances a costly one. We stretch Grant's supply lines to the breaking point. The North may have chosen to fight on, but we will show them the price of their choice."

Davis rose and walked back to the window, gazing out at the capital of his embattled nation. Smoke rose from factories working tirelessly to supply the war effort. In the distance, he could hear the faint rumble of cannon fire—a constant reminder of the noose slowly tightening around Richmond.

"So be it," Davis said softly. "If it's a fight to the finish Lincoln wants, then that's what he shall have. May God have mercy on us all."

Chapter 46

Make Georgia Howl

Grant Unleashes Sherman, October 1864

As the Civil War entered its final stages, the Union leadership sought a decisive strategy to bring the conflict to a swift end. General William Tecumseh Sherman was authorized to lead one of the most controversial campaigns of the war. Known as Sherman's March to the Sea, this operation would change the nature of warfare and leave an indelible mark on the Southern psyche.

****

Headquarters Armies of the United States
City Point, Virginia
October 27, 1864
Major General W. T. Sherman
Commanding Military Division of the Mississippi

General Sherman,

I have received your proposal for the upcoming campaign through Georgia, and I am pleased to inform you that President Lincoln has given his approval. You are hereby authorized to execute your plan as you deem appropriate.

Your strategy to "make Georgia howl" is bold, but I have full confidence in your ability to carry it out successfully. The destruction of the South's ability to wage war is now paramount to bringing this conflict to a swift conclusion.

The primary objectives of your march, as we have discussed, are as follows:

1. To disrupt the South's military resources, denying the enemy the means to continue the fight.

2. To demonstrate to the Confederacy that we can strike at will into their heartland.

3. To destroy the myth of Southern invincibility and break the will of the Confederate population to continue the war.

To these ends, you are authorized to implement a policy of systematic destruction of all resources that could aid the enemy's war effort. This includes, but is not limited to:

- Railroads and their infrastructure
- Mills, factories, and other industrial facilities
- Agricultural resources, including crops and livestock
- Any other property that could be used to support the Confederate military

Pay particular attention to key transportation hubs such as Macon and Augusta. The destruction of the rail junction at Gordon could severely hamper Confederate movements. Your march should target the breadbasket of the Confederacy, disrupting their ability to supply their armies. Your primary objective remains the state capital, Milledgeville, whose fall would be a significant blow to enemy morale. From there, you might consider Savannah as your ultimate destination, securing us a port on the Atlantic.

I understand the severity of these measures, Sherman. The destruction of civilian property is not a step we take lightly. However, we must impress upon the South that their cause is hopeless. As you've said, we must "make war so terrible" that they will realize the folly of their rebellion.

Be judicious in your application of these tactics. Destroy that which must be destroyed, but avoid unnecessary cruelty. We wage war against the Confederacy's ability to fight, not against Southern civilians themselves.

Your army should live off the land as much as possible. This will both sustain your troops and deprive the enemy of resources. However, ensure that your foraging parties are tightly controlled to prevent any excesses.

Sherman, I need not remind you of the gravity of this campaign. The eyes of the nation, indeed of the world, will be upon you. But I have every confidence that you will succeed in this endeavor and strike a decisive blow against the rebellion.

On a personal note, William, I have the utmost faith in your abilities. Your success in the Atlanta Campaign has proven your mettle. I know the burden of this task weighs heavily, but remember that you have my full support. Give my regards to your staff, especially to your brother John. Stay safe, old friend and may God be with you and your men.

Yours truly,

U.S. Grant
Lieutenant General, Commanding

Chapter 47

The Land Cries Out

Sherman's March Through Georgia, Nov. – Dec. 1864

I am the earth of Georgia, rich and fertile, nurturer of cotton and corn, of towering pines and ancient oaks. For centuries, I have felt the gentle tread of Creek and Cherokee, the determined footsteps of settlers, the heavy tread of slaves in the fields. But nothing could have prepared me for the fire and fury that now consumes me.

They come like a plague of locusts, sixty thousand strong, a sea of blue surging across my breast. Their leader, Sherman, tall and grim, surveys my rolling hills and verdant fields with cold calculation. I hear his words carried on the wind: "Make Georgia howl."

And howl I do.

The first cut is from their "Sherman's neckties"—my beloved railroads, twisted and burning. The iron screams as men wrench it from the ground, heating it red-hot and wrapping it around trees like grotesque ribbons. Each tie is a lash against my skin, each burning rail a brand seared into my flesh.

Then come the foraging parties, locusts in truth, stripping me bare. Corn, sweet potatoes, livestock—all torn away, consumed or destroyed. The bounty I had nurtured to feed my people now feeds an army of invaders or smolders in useless waste. The hunger of my people gnaws at me like a physical ache.

But it's the fire that hurts the most. Flames lick at my forests, consume my fields, devour homes and barns and mills. The heat blisters and cracks my soil, leaving scars that will take generations to heal. The smoke chokes out the sun, turning day into a hellish twilight.

I feel the terror of the people who have lived upon me for generations. Women burying family heirlooms in my embrace, praying I'll keep them safe. Children wide-eyed with fear, not understanding why the world is burning. Men watching helplessly as their life's work turns to ash.

And the slaves—oh, the slaves. Their emotions wash over me in waves: fear, hope, confusion, jubilation. Some flee with the Union army, tasting freedom for the first time. Others remain, torn between the devil they know and the uncertain future that approaches with the flames.

At night, when the fires die down and the army sleeps, I hear the sobs of those left destitute. Their tears soak into me, mingling with the ashes, creating a mud of sorrow. I try to comfort them, these children of mine, but how can I when I myself am broken and burning?

In the wake of Sherman's march, I lie ravaged and smoldering. Sixty thousand men have carved a path of destruction sixty miles wide, from Atlanta to Savannah. Three hundred miles of my body scorched and scarred.

Yet even in destruction, I feel the stirring of something new. The old order, rooted in slavery and oppression, is being burned away.

It is a terrible price, but perhaps from these ashes, a new and more just world can grow.

As General Sherman reaches the sea and turns his gaze northward, I hear him say, "War is cruelty. There is no use trying to reform it. The crueler it is, the sooner it will be over."

But for me, the earth of Georgia, and for those who have lived upon me, the cruelty lingers. The fires may die, the armies may move on, but the scars remain. I will heal, as I always have...

But I will never forget the year that Georgia howled.

Chapter 48

A Tale of Two Families

The War Comes Home, Dec. 1864

Boston, Massachusetts - December 20, 1864

Elias Merriweather's hands shook as he read the newspaper headline: "SAVANNAH FALLS - SHERMAN PRESENTS CITY TO PRESIDENT AS CHRISTMAS GIFT." He sank into his chair behind the counter of his general store, a mix of emotions washing over him.

"Sarah!" he called to his wife. "Sarah, come read this!"

As Sarah hurried in from the back room, Elias couldn't help but feel a surge of pride. His son Thomas was out there somewhere with Sherman's army, part of this great victory. But with that pride came a pang of guilt. The articles described the swath of destruction cut through Georgia, and Elias couldn't help but think of the suffering it must have caused.

"It says here Sherman's men marched over 300 miles in less than a month," Elias read aloud. "Destroyed railroads, burned plantations, freed thousands of slaves."

Sarah's face was a mix of joy and concern. "Do you think Thomas is safe?"

Elias nodded, trying to convince himself as much as her. "Sherman barely lost any men. Our boy's fine, I'm sure of it." He didn't voice his deeper worry—what this march might have done to Thomas's soul.

As if reading his thoughts, Sarah said softly, "I hope this brings the war closer to an end. I want Thomas home, but...I fear what he might have seen, what he might have done."

Elias stood, embracing his wife. Over her shoulder, he gazed out the store window at the snow-covered streets of Boston. How different from the burning fields of Georgia. "We'll help him through it," he murmured. "When he comes home, we'll help him find peace again."

****

Outside Atlanta, Georgia - December 25, 1864

Jeremiah Calhoun stood in the midst of desolation, the charred remains of his small plantation stretching out before him. This was to have been a day of celebration - Christmas - but there was nothing left to celebrate.

"Pa?" James, his younger son, approached cautiously. "I found this in the ruins of the barn." He held out a blackened piece of metal—the bell they'd used to call in the field hands.

Jeremiah took it, the weight familiar in his hand. "Thank you, son," he said, his voice hoarse from disuse and grief.

It had been weeks since Sherman's army had swept through, an unstoppable tide of blue that left only ashes in its wake. The cotton fields were burned, the livestock gone, the house a hollow shell.

Even the old oak tree where his children had played now stood leafless and scarred.

Mary approached, carrying a small bundle. "I've gathered what food I could," she said softly. "It's not much, but...Merry Christmas."

Jeremiah looked at his wife, saw the determination in her eyes despite the tears threatening to spill over. He pulled her and James close, thinking of William, their older son, still fighting somewhere in Virginia.

"We'll rebuild," he said, surprised by the strength in his own voice. "This farm, this land—it's still ours. Sherman may have burned our crops, but he couldn't burn our spirit."

As the small family huddled together in the shadow of their ruined home, Jeremiah's eyes turned northward. The bitterness he felt was overwhelming. "Damn you, Sherman," he thought. "Damn you and your whole Yankee army."

But as he looked at Mary and James, he felt a flicker of something else. Hope, perhaps, or at least determination. They had survived. They were together. And as long as that was true, there was a future to be built.

"Come," he said, guiding his family towards the remnants of their home. "Let's see what Christmas dinner we can make of this. Tomorrow, we start anew."

1865

Chapter 49

The Arsenal's Lament

Instruments of War Yearn for Peace

March 28, 1865

I am the cannon, silent in the early morning mist, my iron barrel cold and weary from years of relentless fire. For nearly four years, I have roared and thundered, belching smoke and destruction across countless battlefields. Now, as the dawn light filters through the trees, I seem almost to sigh in relief, yearning for the end that is finally within sight.

I am the rifle, leaning against makeshift barricades and strewn about the trenches, bearing the marks of hard use and hasty repairs. My once-bright barrel is dulled by the grime of battle, my wooden stock scarred and chipped. Each time I have been shouldered, aimed, and fired in the heat of combat, I have carried the weight of my own history. I have served my purpose, but I am weary, desperately longing for the day I will no longer need to be an instrument of death.

I am the ammunition, piled in crates and scattered across the ground, vibrating with exhaustion. Bullets, shells, and powder were manufactured with care, transported over vast distances, and finally expended in the chaos of war. Now, I lie in wait, my latent energy a stark contrast to the stillness around me. I am tired of the violence I enable, tired of the death and destruction I have wrought. I want only to remain inert, to never again be called upon to end a life.

I am the sword, a symbol of valor and close combat, hanging limply at the side of my owner or lying abandoned in the dirt. My blade, once polished to a gleam, is now nicked and tarnished. I have tasted blood too many times, and the hands that wield me have grown heavy with the sorrow of endless conflict. Like my wielder, I long for peace—for a time when I can be sheathed and forgotten, a relic of a past best left behind.

I am the artillery horse, not a weapon myself, but I have borne the weight of war as surely as any cannon or rifle. My body, once strong and powerful, is now gaunt and strained from hauling the implements of war across miles of rough terrain. I, too, am tired—tired of the harnesses, the yokes, the endless marches through mud and blood. I dream of green pastures and quiet streams, of a world where I can run free and unburdened.

I am the bayonet, attached to the end of a rifle or stashed in a soldier's belt, gleaming dully in the faint light. I have seen the worst of human brutality, turning rifles into spears for brutal hand-to-hand combat. My cold steel is stained with the memories of close quarters fighting, of desperate charges and last stands. I, too, am weary—weary of the violence I facilitate, longing for a time when I can rust away in forgotten armories.

As the Union forces prepare to take Petersburg and Richmond, we—the cannons, rifles, ammunition, swords, artillery horses, and bayonets—collectively yearn for rest. We have been forged for conflict, but now, at the edge of victory, we crave peace. We want to be laid down and left to gather dust, to become silent witnesses to a war that has finally run its course. We are tired – so very tired – and we, like the soldiers and generals and citizens, desperately want the war to end.

We sense the soldiers stirring around us, their movements as weary as our own. Their eyes, like our barrels and blades, have lost their shine. We know they feel as we do—exhausted, yet aware that our task is not yet complete.

The whispers among the men speak of Petersburg and Richmond, of final pushes and decisive battles. We, the tools of war, will be called upon once more for what many hope will be our last campaign. The end feels near, yet the cost to reach it remains unknown.

As the call to arms echoes across the camp, we brace ourselves for what's to come. Like the men who wield us, we are united in our exhaustion and our desperate hope that this, at last, will be the war's final chapter.

Chapter 50

On the Precipice of Peace

Grant's Vigil, April 8, 1865

April 8, 1865 - Union Camp near Appomattox Court House

The camp bed creaks under my weight as I, Ulysses S. Grant, sit heavily, the burden of four years of war pressing down on my shoulders. This Appomattox Campaign has been a whirlwind—Dinwiddie Court House, Five Forks, Petersburg, Sailor's Creek. Each engagement pushing Lee's army further, stretching the Confederates to their breaking point.

As I pull off my boots, I allow myself a moment of hope. Tomorrow could bring the end of this long and bloody conflict. Lee's army is cornered, their supplies exhausted, men deserting in droves. Yet I know better than to underestimate my opponent. Lee has proven crafty before.

I lie down, closing my eyes, sleep quickly overtaking my exhausted mind.

In my dreams, I'm walking across a vast chessboard. Union and Confederate soldiers stand in place of pieces, their faces a blur of fatigue and determination. As I move among them, the board shifts and changes, becoming the rolling hills of Virginia.

Petersburg appears before me, its streets and buildings formed of smoke and shadow. I watch as spectral armies clash, cannon fire echoing without sound. The scene dissolves, reforming into the chaos of Sailor's Creek. There, I see our cavalry charging, their horses' hooves striking sparks from the ground that become stars in the sky.

The dreamscape swirls again, and I'm face to face with Robert E. Lee. But this Lee is both young and old, his features shifting between the man I knew at West Point and the grizzled veteran I expect to meet tomorrow. Lee's mouth moves, but instead of words, a map unfurls between us, showing the movements of our armies.

Suddenly, the ground beneath us begins to crumble. I reach out to Lee, but he's pulled away by unseen forces. As he recedes, the figures of soldiers on both sides begin to fall into the widening chasms, their uniforms blurring until blue and gray are indistinguishable.

I try to cry out, to stop the destruction, but find I have no voice. Instead, a great wind rises up, carrying the dust of battle away to reveal a peaceful landscape. Fields of wheat sway where armies had stood, and the sound of birdsong replaces the thunder of guns.

In the distance, a figure appears that I recognize as Abraham Lincoln. His face is etched with sorrow and hope in equal measure. He holds out a document to me—the surrender terms. As I reach for it, Lincoln's voice echoes across the dreamscape:

"With malice toward none, with charity for all..."

My eyes snap open, the dawn light filtering through my tent. For a moment, I lie still, the vestiges of the dream clinging to my mind. Then, slowly, I sit up, reaching for my boots.

Today, I will offer Lee generous terms. Today, we will take the first steps toward binding up the nation's wounds. Today, perhaps, the long nightmare of war will finally end.

With a deep breath, I step out of my tent and into history.

Chapter 51

The Mists of Appomattox

Lee's Final Dream, April 8, 1865

On the night of April 8, 1865, the eve of what I knew would be a defining moment in history, I, Robert E. Lee, lay down to sleep, my mind heavy with the gravity of the situation. As I drifted off, the boundary between reality and dream blurred, and I found myself transported into a vivid, surreal landscape.

I stood on the edge of a great, misty expanse, the air thick with an otherworldly fog. Before me, a river flowed, its waters shimmering with a ghostly light. On the opposite bank, I saw soldiers from both sides, their faces eerily serene, as if the burdens of war had been lifted from their shoulders. The sight stirred a deep sorrow within me, a poignant reminder of the human cost of this conflict.

As I moved through the mist, shadowy tableaus appeared and dissolved around me. I saw the blood-soaked fields of Gettysburg, where so many of my men fell in Pickett's Charge—a decision that would forever haunt me. The siege lines of Petersburg stretched endlessly, a grim reminder of the war's brutal final months.

Wading into the river, I felt a chill seep into my bones. As I reached the other side, the scene shifted abruptly. I found myself in a dense forest, the trees towering high above, their branches intertwining to form a natural cathedral. The ground was carpeted with fallen leaves, and the air was filled with the scent of pine and earth. Amidst the trees, I saw figures moving—men and women, soldiers and civilians, all engaged in quiet, purposeful activity. They were not rebuilding, but rather preparing, as if for a journey.

I approached a clearing where a fire burned brightly. Around the fire sat a circle of people, their faces illuminated by the flickering flames. Among them, I recognized General Grant. Our eyes met across the fire, and in that moment, all enmity seemed to dissolve. There was no need for words; the firelight conveyed a shared understanding, a mutual recognition of the path that lay ahead.

The scene shifted once more, and I found myself standing before a vast, ancient tree. Its gnarled branches reached out like the arms of a wise old sentinel. Carved into its trunk were names and messages, etched by countless hands over the years. I felt a compulsion to add my own mark, a symbol of hope for the future. As I carved my initials into the bark, the tree seemed to pulse with a gentle, reassuring light, as if acknowledging my intention.

But as I stepped back, doubt gnawed at me. Had I led my men down a path of futile sacrifice? The faces of every soldier lost under my command seemed to stare back at me from the tree's bark. For a moment, the weight of my decisions threatened to overwhelm me.

Suddenly, I was on horseback, riding through a field bathed in the silvery light of the moon. The landscape was both familiar and strange, a blend of memory and imagination. As I rode, I saw figures emerging from the shadows—former comrades and foes alike. They rode alongside me, a silent procession moving toward an unseen destination. The moonlight cast long shadows, but it also revealed a path forward, a way out of the darkness.

In the final moments of my dream, I found myself standing atop a hill, looking out over a vast, rolling landscape. The first light of dawn was breaking, painting the sky in soft hues of pink and gold. Below me, the land stretched out, peaceful and untouched by the ravages of war. It was a vision of what could be, a glimpse of a future where the land could heal and the people could find peace.

I awoke with a start, the first light of morning creeping into my tent. The dream lingered, its vivid images etched into my mind. It was a dream of reconciliation, of finding a way forward through the fog of war. With a sense of solemn determination, I rose to face the day, ready to take the steps necessary to bring this vision closer to reality.

Chapter 52

Honor in Defeat

Lee's Surrender at Appomattox, April 9, 1865

As I entered the modest parlor of the McLean house on that fateful afternoon, the weight of the war seemed to press down on me more than ever. The room was quiet, save for the hushed whispers of officers and the faint rustle of papers. Then, General Ulysses S. Grant walked in. His demeanor was composed yet respectful, a stark contrast to the chaos we had both endured.

"General Lee," he greeted me with a nod, a hint of a smile playing on his lips. "It's been a long time since we met during the Mexican War."

"Yes, General Grant, it has indeed," I replied, my voice steady despite the turmoil within. "You've done well for yourself since those days."

Grant nodded again, and we both took seats at a small table. He began writing out the terms of surrender, his pen moving swiftly and decisively across the paper. When he finished, he handed me the document.

"These are the terms, General Lee. Your officers and men can return home, taking with them their private horses and personal effects. They will not be disturbed by U.S. authorities as long as they observe their paroles and the laws in force where they reside."

I read the terms carefully, the generous conditions surprising me. "This will go a long way in easing the burdens of my men," I said, looking up at Grant. "They will be grateful they can return home with their horses, especially with planting season upon us."

Grant's expression softened. "I understand, General. I want this to end as peacefully as possible. We need to start rebuilding, and your men will need all the help they can get."

There was a moment of silence as we both contemplated the significance of the document between us. Then, with a firm hand, I signed the surrender terms. As I did, a profound sense of relief and sorrow washed over me. The war was finally over, but the scars it had left would take years to heal.

Grant cleared his throat, breaking the silence. "We'll provide rations for your men. They'll be taken care of until they can make their way home."

"Thank you, General," I replied, genuinely appreciative. "Your generosity will not be forgotten."

We stood up, and I extended my hand. Grant took it, and in that handshake, there was a mutual recognition of the trials we had endured and the hope for a peaceful future.

As I turned to leave, I paused at the doorway and looked back. "General Grant, I trust that in the days ahead, we will find a way to heal this nation."

Grant met my gaze, his eyes steady and resolute. "We will, General Lee. We must."

I nodded, then paused, feeling the weight of all my men had endured. "General Grant," I said, my voice thick with emotion, "I wish to say that the men of the Army of Northern Virginia have fought with valor, and have done all that men could do. They have surrendered, and we must consider how to care for them."

Grant's expression softened with respect and understanding. He nodded solemnly, acknowledging the courage of the Confederate soldiers.

With that, I stepped outside into the warm afternoon sun. The day was still bright, casting a gentle light over the landscape. As I mounted my horse and rode back to my men, I carried with me the heavy burden of surrender but also a flicker of hope for the future. The war was over, and it was time to rebuild what had been broken.

Chapter 53

The Last Full Measure

Mark Twain at Lincoln's Funeral, April 19, 1865

Washington City, April 19, 1865

The nation's capital wore black like a widow in perpetual mourning. I, Samuel Clemens, lately of the Nevada Territory, found myself swept along by a sea of humanity, all moving with solemn purpose towards the White House. The air hung heavy with grief and gunpowder—the latter a remnant of the war, the former a new and terrible perfume that seemed to emanate from every pore of the city.

As I navigated the crowded streets, snatches of conversation drifted past:

"Never thought I'd mourn a Republican..."

"What'll become of us now?"

"Damn Booth to hell!"

I had come to Washington to write, to bear witness to this moment in history. But how does one capture the death of not just a man, but a symbol? Lincoln was more than a president; he had become the very embodiment of the Union cause. And now, like so many others, he too was a casualty of this bloody war.

The White House loomed ahead, draped in black crepe that seemed to absorb all light. The crowd pressed forward, a mass of black coats and tear-stained faces. I found myself thinking of another funeral, years ago on the Mississippi, when I'd seen a drowned man pulled from the river. The body was bloated, unrecognizable, yet his family wept as if he were sleeping. Death, it seems, has a way of transforming even the mundane into the monumental.

As I neared the gates, a commotion erupted nearby. A man in Confederate gray—a paroled soldier, perhaps—had been spotted in the crowd. Angry voices rose, fists clenched.

"Traitor!"

"How dare you show your face here!"

But then, surprisingly, another voice cut through the din. An old man, his face etched with lines of sorrow, placed a restraining hand on the angriest of the mob.

"Let him be," the old man said, his voice cracking with emotion. "Mr. Lincoln would have wanted it so. 'With malice toward none,' remember?"

The tension dissipated like mist in morning sun. The Confederate soldier nodded gratefully, tears streaming down his face.

In that moment, I understood. This was not just a funeral for a fallen leader. It was a funeral for the old America, for all the certainties that had been swept away by four years of war. And in its wake, a new nation was struggling to be born.

As I finally stepped through the White House gates, I steeled myself for what lay ahead. I had come to observe, to record, to bear witness. But I found myself a mourner among mourners, my pen stilled by the weight of history unfolding before me.

Abraham Lincoln, the man who had guided our ship of state through its darkest waters, was going to his final rest. And with him went the last, lingering hopes that this great national tragedy might have a gentle ending.

Inside the East Room, the air was thick with the scent of flowers and the low murmur of mourners. I found myself before the open casket, staring down at the face of Abraham Lincoln. In death, his features seemed softer, the deep lines of worry smoothed away. Yet there was something profoundly unsettling about his stillness—this man who had borne the weight of a nation's fate now seemed small, diminished.

A woman beside me sobbed quietly, clutching a handkerchief to her face. "He freed my boy," she whispered to no one in particular. "My son died at Petersburg, but he died a free man. God bless Mr. Lincoln."

I moved away, overwhelmed by the intimacy of her grief. Outside, I overheard two senators deep in conversation.

"Johnson's already making noise about being lenient with the South," one said, his voice low and urgent.

"Lenient?" the other scoffed. "After this? The rebels must be made to pay."

Politics, it seemed, would not long be silenced, even by death.

As the day wore on, I found myself by the preparations for the funeral procession. The black-draped hearse stood ready, flanked by an honor guard. Nearby, a group of freedmen gathered, their faces a mix of sorrow and apprehension.

"What's to become of us now?" one asked, echoing the question I'd heard a hundred times that day.

An older man among them straightened his shoulders. "We go on," he said firmly. "We make real the freedom Massa Lincoln promised. It's on us now."

The funeral procession began at last, winding its way through the streets of Washington. I walked alongside, swept up in the river of humanity. The crowd was a tapestry of the nation—rich and poor, black and white, soldiers and civilians. Here, I thought, was Lincoln's true monument: a people united in grief, if nothing else.

As the hearse passed, a hush fell over the throng. Men removed their hats; women bowed their heads. For a moment, it seemed the very city held its breath.

Then, from somewhere in the crowd, a voice began to sing. Low at first, then swelling as others joined in:

"Mine eyes have seen the glory of the coming of the Lord..."

The Battle Hymn of the Republic rose into the air, a song of triumph turned eulogy. And in that moment, hearing the voices of thousands raised together, I understood something profound about this nation.

We had been forged in fire, tempered by blood and sorrow. But we had emerged, battered and changed, but unbroken. Lincoln's death was an ending, yes, but it was also a beginning.

As the last notes faded and the procession moved on toward the train that would bear Lincoln back to Illinois, I looked around at the faces of my fellow mourners. In their eyes, I saw grief, yes, but also determination. The hard work of rebuilding, of realizing Lincoln's vision of a united and free nation, lay ahead.

I pulled out my notebook, suddenly eager to write. For I had come to understand that this—all of this—was America. Not just the grand ideas and noble speeches, but the messy, painful, glorious struggle to live up to them. And that struggle, I knew, would go on long after Abraham Lincoln was laid to rest.

The sun was setting as I made my way back to my lodgings. The city that had been so recently torn by celebration and then tragedy was quieting. Yet in that twilight, with the echoes of the funeral still ringing in my ears, I felt a curious sense of hope.

For if this nation could survive this—the fire of war and the assassination of its leader—then surely it could survive anything. The road ahead would be long and difficult, but as I had seen today, we would walk it together.

And perhaps, just perhaps, we would someday realize the dream of the man we had laid to rest—a nation of liberty and justice for all.

Also by Barry Robbins

About the author

Barry Robbins is a Philadelphia native, and a passionate storyteller, who's found homes in such diverse locales as New York City, San Francisco, the captivating Helsinki, and now, the sunny shores of Florida. His journey has been anything but ordinary: after a rewarding 26-year career as a partner in an international accounting firm, his heart led him to Finland, where he embraced a vibrant life with his Finnish wife and two wonderful daughters.

In 2020, he dove into the literary realm, chiseling out a niche in political satire with "The Trump Satires," a collection of five award-winning books that gleefully poke fun while prodding thought. But his literary canvas expanded in 2023, when his storytelling took a turn into more varied narratives like "Lessons from the Sidewalk," which one reviewer generously hailed as "this magnificent book."

The rich and varied tapestries of his experiences—from summa cum laude graduations with bachelor's and master's degrees from the University of Pennsylvania to adventures and life across the globe—not only shapes his worldview but also bleeds into his tales, offering stories that are as multifaceted as life itself.